YOURS BY CHRISTMAS

JENNIFER YOUNGBLOOD

ARBOR
HOUSE

GET YOUR FREE BOOK

Get Beastly Charm: A Contemporary retelling of beauty & the beast as a welcome gift when you sign up for my newsletter. You'll get information on my new releases, book recommendations, discounts, and other freebies.

Get the book at:

http://bit.ly/freebookjenniferyoungblood

PROLOGUE

It was the kind of cold that would freeze a person's toes and fingers off. In another time and place, Beckett wouldn't have spent more than thirty minutes outside. Tonight, however, he was grateful for the cold. It sank through the holes of his worn shoes, moving up his legs and torso like morphine, numbing his aching heart. The cold snuffed out the fire raging in his head—the voice that screamed of his failures and how any path to redemption was forever barred. He trudged through the snow, oblivious to the trash littering the sidewalk or the bars covering the windows of the aging buildings. The sights and stench of the streets would've horrified him before, when he was donning two-thousand-dollar suits and driving a Lexus to his high-rise office in the center of downtown Salt Lake City. Now, it was as commonplace as breathing. The frigid wind picked up. He pulled his thin coat tighter around him as he tucked his chin into his neck and plodded forward.

Normally, Beckett's senses were dulled to the point where he hardly remembered the life he lived before. Alcohol was the great cure-all. If he drank enough of it, he could hardly remember his own name. Today, however, was different. Today was Jasmine's birthday. She was turning seven today. Beckett didn't want to think about

Jasmine with her happy, rosy cheeks and cocoa-colored ringlets. The trusting look in her deep brown eyes. The lilt in her voice when she called him daddy. Jasmine wanted a pink Barbie cake with sparkles. Tears pressed against his eyes as he swallowed. Unbidden scenes from the accident flashed before his eyes, the guilt knotting his gut.

It had been a normal day. Pressures at the office were increasing. Beckett was always behind. Nothing he did was enough to satisfy his bulldog boss. Before darting out of his office to pick up Jasmine from her dance class, he'd taken a few swigs out of the flask he kept hidden beneath a stack of files in his bottom desk drawer. One minute he was driving, the road a blur, Jasmine chattering about a new dance she'd learned. The next minute, everything changed. Beckett felt the blunt force of the crash the same instant he heard the sickening sound of crunching metal. Then came the worst—Jasmine's terrified screams that gave way to intermittent whimpers. He'd called 911, screaming into the phone. It seemed to take forever before the wail of the sirens pierced the night air.

A few hours later, in a sterile hospital waiting room, a grim-faced doctor would deliver the blow. Jasmine's ankle had been crushed. It would require multiple surgeries, and there was a chance she'd never walk again. Melinda's face had crumpled, tears streaming down her cheeks. As Beckett went to hug her, she pushed him away, condemnation burning in her eyes. "This is all your fault!" she spat.

"Please, Melinda." His voice had cracked with desperation. "I— I'm sorry. I never meant—" He reached for her again.

She got up in his face. "I can smell the alcohol on your breath." For an instant, Beckett saw something in her eyes—a sliver of the love they'd once shared. Before he could blink, however, her eyes went flatter than dull pennies as she turned her back to him and walked away.

It was then that he'd known, he was dead to her. He loosened his silk tie and threw it into the garbage on his way out of the hospital.

That was six months ago.

He wet his dry lips, the thirst for a drink rising in him like a greedy vulture demanding to be satisfied. He paused and leaned against the side of a building, removing the bottle from inside his coat. Beckett took a long swig, appreciating how the liquid burned down his throat. Another couple of drinks helped ease the pain. The snow was falling harder, large blobs coating everything in white. Cars moved along the streets like cautious snails, trying to avoid contact. The world felt still, like he was in one of those snow globes Jasmine loved. Beckett's breath pushed out a warm mist against the air as he continued to his destination.

Fifteen minutes later, he went in through the backdoor of a shelter. A middle-aged, portly man with a tapered salt and pepper beard was sitting behind a metal desk, chewing on a pencil as he stared at the screen of his laptop. When he saw Beckett, he waved in recognition as he stood, pulling his pants over his belly. "Hey, Blanket Man. I wondered what time you'd show up here." He went to a nearby counter and picked up a stack of blankets, depositing them in Beckett's arms. "It's a cold one tonight. The temperature's falling into single digits."

"Yes."

"I'm sure there'll be plenty of people who can use these blankets. Some ladies from a local church dropped them off today. It's mighty kind of you to deliver them. After you get done passing these out, there are plenty more."

Beckett nodded. This was how the conversation always went, with Scotty making small talk and Beckett throwing in a few short answers and nods. Scotty didn't seem to mind that Beckett didn't want to talk. He was always pleasant, and he looked Beckett in the eye when he spoke to him. Most people didn't. The homeless moved through the city like faceless ghosts, scavenging what they could to survive.

"Oh, by the way, I reserved you a spot at the shelter tonight. It's too cold to be outside."

"Thank you." Beckett's hands ached from the cold. He'd had a pair of gloves once, but they were long gone.

"Tell everyone you see that they need to get indoors." Scotty's mouth turned down in a frown as he pulled at his beard. "This is the kind of weather that kills people."

If only Beckett could be so lucky. Death was preferable to his miserable existence. Several times, he'd looked up at the tops of the buildings, thinking how easy it would be to just jump and end it all. He didn't know what was keeping him here. Maybe it was cowardice. Even now, he craved life and the bottle. Maybe it was Jasmine. His heart clutched as he pushed the thoughts away. He no longer had a wife or daughter. He was a nobody.

With the blankets in hand, Beckett went out the door. After the warmth of the shelter, the night felt colder. He suppressed a shiver, forcing himself to embrace the cold as his feet worked through the snow. His first stop was a group of four men at a nearby park. They were sitting on the ground, huddled close together, their backs resting against a waist-high concrete wall.

"It's Blanket Man," an older man named Beaker exclaimed in a hoarse voice. No one went by their real names on the streets. They used names that fit the person's personality or features. Beaker had a large, pitted nose. He held up a gnarly hand. "Join the party," he said glibly. "It's a little cold, but what can ya do?" He laughed at his own joke.

Slim Jim, sitting next to him, barked out a raspy smoker laugh, his thin shoulders shaking. "Yep, we're having us a party." He raised a hopeful eye to Beckett. "Got anything to drink?"

"Or a cigarette?" a young man with greasy hair and glassy eyes asked.

A pang shot through Beckett. The kid was a newcomer. He couldn't be more than eighteen or nineteen years old. His face was gaunt, his eyes ringed in hollow circles. It seemed such a shame for him to be here, strung out on drugs. Even as the thought ran through his mind, Beckett laughed inwardly. He, of all people, had no room to judge. No one on the streets would ever imagine that he used to be an executive at one of the most prestigious financial advisory firms in Salt Lake. Out here, he was a scruffy drunk who delivered blankets to those who didn't have the presence of mind to seek shelter when the temperatures plummeted. He didn't really know why he felt compelled to go out night after night, delivering blankets. Maybe it was a form of atonement for his past sins. All he knew was that he couldn't seem to rest until the blankets were handed out.

"Nope, sorry. I'm all out of both," Beckett lied, "but I do come bearing gifts." No way was he sharing his booze. He'd spent a full day cleaning trash out of a yard to earn the money to buy this bottle. He handed them each a blanket. "It's supposed to be down in the single digits tonight," he said, repeating Scotty's words. "It might be wise to get to a shelter." The cold seeped into his bones, making him feel sluggish.

Beaker waved a hand. "Nah, too crowded. We'll be all right."

The young man started singing a song about them being all right.

"Suit yourselves." Beckett moved on to the next stop, passing out more blankets. He suspected that a few of the people were so far gone in their minds that they didn't even realize they were cold. One man was holding an animated conversation with an imaginary person, laughing one second and shouting curses the next. Maybe Beckett would end up that way—not having a clue who he even was. When the blankets were gone he returned to the shelter, intent on making one more round before hunkering down for the night.

"Hey," Scotty said, "you're back."

Beckett gave a curt nod of acknowledgement and went to the counter, picking up an armful of blankets.

Scotty touched his beard. "Uh, Beckett, before you head back out, there's someone here to see you."

Beckett frowned, hearing his own name. Not once, in all the times he'd come to this shelter to pick up blankets, had Scotty called him by his real name. Up until now, Beckett hadn't even realized that Scotty knew his name. Suspicion stirred inside him. "Who is it?" he demanded. It had better not be his former boss! Jack Bisson had come lurking around once, about a month after Beckett had thrown in the towel. He urged Beckett to check himself into a rehab center, saying he'd even pay for the treatment. "Think of your wife and daughter," Jack had said. "With Jasmine's ankle in such bad shape, she needs you now more than ever." Beckett laughed in his face, telling the pompous man in no uncertain terms exactly what he thought of him. Had Jack shown him an ounce of compassion when Beckett was working, instead of riding his case 24/7, Beckett might not have turned to alcohol. Then, he never would've been drinking the night he picked Jasmine up from her dance class, and he wouldn't have had the car accident that shattered her ankle. Beckett balled his fist, squeezing the blankets. He'd refrained from punching Jack Bisson in the face the last time he showed up. This time, Bisson wouldn't be so lucky. "Where's Bisson?" he growled.

Scotty frowned. "I'm not sure who that is." He scooted back his chair and stood, his eyes resting on the blankets in Beckett's arms. "Maybe you should put those down and follow me."

Reluctantly, Beckett complied. When they entered the large common room, Beckett scanned the crowd of people, packed like sardines into every available inch of floor space. When he saw them across the room, his breath froze in his throat. He couldn't do it! His eyes narrowed as he spun around to Scotty. "What is this?"

Scotty held up a hand. "Your wife and daughter have gone to great lengths to find you. The least you can do is hear them out." He lowered his voice. "I know your history, Beckett. That you're a good man. You had a career, a wonderful family. That man is still in there. You just have to find him."

Beckett let out a harsh laugh. "If I were a good man, my daughter wouldn't be in a wheelchair." Tears rose in his eyes as he cleared his throat and swallowed. He'd lost count of the number of times he'd dreamed of seeing Jasmine over the past few months. A hot anger coursed through his veins. Melinda had no right to bring Jasmine here. Maybe she wanted Jasmine to see firsthand how far her dad had fallen. Everything in him wanted to turn around and flee as far from here as he could get.

"Daddy!" Jasmine's face lit up as she waved.

Too late to run. Beckett sighed in resignation as he forced his feet to move forward. When he reached them, he stood there awkwardly, at a loss for words. Melinda's pinched face said it all—that he was an embarrassment. Melinda had always been concerned about social status and the image they portrayed to the world. He could only imagine what she must think of his ragged clothes, scraggly beard, grimy fingernails, his unwashed stench. He was a walking skeleton, a shadow of his former self.

Jasmine was beaming. She seemed oblivious to the change in him. "I've missed you so much." She held out her hands for him to hug her. Beckett's feet stayed rooted to the floor. He wanted to hug her, but life on the streets had hardened him to the point where personal contact seemed foreign. Finally, he patted her hand instead. She was soft, untouched by the ugliness of the streets.

"Good to see you, pretty girl." His eyes settled on the cast, visible beneath her sweat pants. He hated himself in that moment, wished he could disappear into nothing. How dare Melinda bring Jasmine here! He wanted Jasmine to remember him as he was before. Not now, consumed by his vice. He glared at Melinda. "What're you doing here?" Melinda looked thinner than he remembered, her face drawn and pale. It seemed like it had been another life when he'd loved her.

Melinda lifted her chin, a protective hand going over Jasmine's shoulder. "I came here because of Jazzie," she said stiffly. "It was her birthday wish."

Jasmine gave him a searching look. "Come home with us, Daddy." Her voice cracked. "Please."

"For her sake," Melinda added. "You need help." Her jaw tightened. "It's bad enough that Jasmine's going through all the pain and suffering of her ankle. Must she lose her father too?" The words came out in short, angry bursts. She gave him a hard, resentful look. "You're being selfish."

Tears bubbled in Jasmine's eyes, her lower lip trembling. "Please, Daddy, come home. We miss you."

Selfish! Loser! Drunk! Beckett's head felt like it was splitting in two. Oh, how he wished he could relive that dreadful night of the accident, that he could go back and nip the drinking in the bud before it turned into a hideous monster. He thought of the bottle beneath his coat, the need for a drink overwhelming. He hated this—loathed his weakness. Tears pooled in his eyes. Beckett Bradshaw was an illusion.

There was nothing left of that man except pain and regret. "I'm sorry," he uttered as he fled.

The last thing he heard before he darted out the door into the cold was Jazzie's anguished cry. "Daddy!"

———

BECKETT'S MIND was a blur as he wandered aimlessly in the snow. After he'd drained the bottle of booze, he found himself at the train station downtown. When the train stopped, he got on and slumped down in a seat. As the train moved forward, he forced his mind to go blank, drifting in the pleasant stupor of his drunken state. He didn't know how long he'd traveled before a transit officer got on, checking tickets. It would only be a matter of minutes before the officer got to him. He'd be thrown off the train, possibly spend a night in jail. He hoped for the latter where at least it'd be warm. Earlier, he'd not minded the cold, but now that he was warm, he wanted to stay that way a while longer. He tensed as the officer stood beside the woman sitting in front of Beckett. She was also homeless. Beckett could tell from her shabby clothes, stooped posture, and the broken aura the woman exuded. He knew all of this because he was the same.

"May I see your ticket, ma'am?" the officer asked.

The woman only grunted.

When the officer asked again, she just sat there, her posture stiff, belligerent.

"Ma'am, I need you to come with me." The officer went to grab her hand, but she hurled out a few insults and took a swing that caught the officer square in the face. To be so old and shriveled, the woman was feisty. A scuffle ensued, which lasted about five seconds, until the transit officer had the woman in cuffs, hauling her to her feet. She turned to Beckett and winked like they shared some secret joke. She was probably crazy, imagining he was someone else. At the next stop, the officer pulled the woman off.

Beckett breathed a sigh of relief as the train moved forward. He glanced outside at the swirling snow. There was at least a foot of accumulation on the ground. He pulled his coat around him. It felt good to be warm. His mind got lost in the movement of the train. Beckett was barely cognizant of his motions when his eyelids grew heavy, his chin falling into his chest. The next thing he knew, someone was standing over him, shaking his arm.

He jerked, sitting up.

"It's time to get off the train," a woman in a uniform said irritably. "It's the end of the line."

He looked around, realizing the train was empty except for him and the woman. She must've been driving the train.

"Thanks," he mumbled as he stood and got off. He winced, shrinking into himself, when a cold blast of wind hit him in the face, nearly taking his breath away. Snowflakes flew into his mouth. He spit them out, tucking his face into his neck. The snow was coming down so hard he could barely see. He wasn't even sure where he was. Maybe it didn't matter.

As he walked, his mind seemed to take flight. He thought of the day Jasmine was born, the thrill he felt when he held her for the first time. Then his mind flitted to the day he got hired at W. Shields Financial Corp. The new job came with all the bells and whistles. By all accounts, he and Melinda had made it. Two short months later, they moved into a new house in an exclusive Draper neighborhood.

His hands shoved in his pockets, Beckett left the lights of the station, welcoming the darkness of the rural road. With every step, he got the feeling of being alone on an alien planet. It was just him, not another soul in sight. The snow had stopped. The thin glow from the moon and stars was his only light. His feet and hands were numb with cold as he trudged on, losing all track of time and space.

Two lights up ahead shined through the darkness. He walked toward the lights. When he got closer, he realized they were off to the side of the road. A jolt went through him. The lights were from an overturned car. Curiosity prompted him to take a closer look.

The accident looked bad, the top of the car crushed like a tin can. Hearing a cry, he looked to his right realizing there was a person lying in the snow. His stomach roiled. Someone had been thrown out of the car.

"Help!" a feeble voice said.

He edged closer. A woman lifted her hand. "Help me, please."

He tensed, then a roar started in his head. Time rolled back, and he was at his accident. He felt the force of the impact. The woman's cries became Jasmine's cries. "No!" he shouted, his hands going over his ears. "I didn't mean to hurt you." A sob broke through his throat. "Please forgive me, Jazzie!" He moved to walk away.

"Don't leave me here," the woman begged. "Help me. I think my leg is broken. My head's bleeding. I'm hurting." Her voice sounded small and childlike.

Tears coursed down his face, reality coming back to him. The woman was hurt. He needed to help. He glanced around. "Was anyone else in the car?"

"No, just me," she croaked, then coughed to clear her throat.

"Do you have a phone?"

The woman laughed futilely. "Yeah, somewhere in my car."

Beckett's eyes rested on the mangled car. No way would be able to get inside to find the phone.

"I'm so c—cold," the woman said, her teeth chattering.

She could die of hypothermia. Beckett knelt beside her, taking an assessment. The woman was older, in her mid or late sixties. A wave of nausea rolled over him when he realized her leg was turned at an awkward angle. No way could he move her. He thought of the blankets at the shelter, wishing he had one now. He removed his coat and placed it over her. He hugged his arms, fighting off a shiver as the wind cut through his shirt.

Not knowing what else to do, he sat down behind her. As carefully as he could, he lifted her head and scooted in so her head could rest against his chest. She grunted in pain at the movement. "I'm sorry. I'm just moving close to you so our body heat can work in our favor." He felt the stickiness of her blood, looked down at her matted hair. Would she bleed out before help arrived?

"You don't have a phone?" the woman asked, her voice coated with desperation.

"No." He hated dashing her hopes.

"Maybe you should get back in your car and go get help."

"I don't have a car. I was out walking when I saw your car."

The woman started crying. "I'm going to die out here, aren't I?"

"No," he reassured her. "I can go get help." He tried to think. How far had he walked from the train station?

She clutched his arm. "Don't leave me alone." Her voice broke. "You can't leave me."

"Okay. I'll stay right here. You're gonna be okay." An incredulous laugh built in Beckett's throat. He couldn't guarantee the woman anything, yet there was no sense in causing her more alarm. His mind spun. Man, he needed a drink. He swallowed hard, pushing away the thirst. He needed to focus. This woman's life was at risk. Blood seeped into his shirt. He had to stop the bleeding. "Hang tight." He shifted slightly and pulled out the bottom of his plaid shirt, tearing off a large section. Carefully, he wound it around her head and tied it. From what Beckett could tell, the makeshift bandage was helping. He felt a fraction of relief when heat from her seeped into him, and he knew it was doing the same for her. He'd keep her warm until help arrived.

"What's your name?" the woman asked.

"Beckett."

Silence lapsed between them as he looked up at the twinkling stars.

"Thank you for staying with me." The words drifted up, getting lost in the still of the night.

"Of course. What's your name?"

"Sadie."

He looked at the car. "What happened?"

"I hit a patch of ice, and the car skidded out of control. I wasn't wearing a seatbelt. When I came to, I was out here, hurting all over." Her voice caught. "I've been out here for a while, praying for help. Then, you showed up."

The idea of him being an answer to someone's prayer evoked conflicting emotions inside him.

"Why are you out here on a night like this?"

He chuckled. "It's a long story."

"I seem to have plenty of time," she said morosely. "Listening to you will help me take my mind off the pain." She winced. "I need something to focus on."

"All right." He smiled thinly. "You'd never know it by looking at me now, but at one time I was somebody." The words tumbled out almost faster than he could speak them, as if his heart needed to empty everything out. He told Sadie about his hopes and insatiable ambition, how his desire to chase down the dream took a wrong turn when he buckled under the stress of being a hedge fund manager and lost a substantial amount of his clients' money. He spoke of Melinda and how they slowly drifted apart until there was nothing left to build on. Tears rolled from his eyes when he spoke of the accident and Jasmine. How today was her birthday and she'd come to the shelter. "After everything I've done, Jazzie looked at me with such love, begging me to come home. I wanted to so badly." His voice shook. "I just don't know how." As his admission flowed into the night air, he felt the futileness of his words.

Sadie grasped his arm, and he was surprised by her strength. "I'll make you a deal."

He'd gotten so caught up in telling his story, that for an instant, he'd forgotten he was here with this woman who was valiantly clinging to life. "Okay," he said warily.

"You get your life cleaned up, and I'll survive this."

He laughed. "Trust me, I would if I could."

"Prayer helps."

God seemed as distant from Beckett as the lonely stars above. Where was God when he had the accident that crushed Jasmine's ankle? Where was God when he gave up all hope and succumbed to his demons? "Yeah, it's a nice notion, but I dunno."

"It's more than a notion." Conviction rang in her voice. "God sent you here to help me tonight. If you pray for help and trust in Him, He'll help you."

Something stirred within his heart, as an unexpected warmth seeped over him. Was it possible? Could he really change?

"What do you say, Beckett? Do we have a deal?" Her voice broke. "Please, I need this to make it through."

"All right," he finally said to placate her. "Tell me about you," he prompted to change the subject.

She let out a low chuckle. "Oh, you don't wanna hear about me." Her breathing was labored and shallow. She grunted in pain, then whimpered. A feeling of helplessness came over Beckett. He didn't want Sadie to die. He looked up at the sky and did something he thought he'd never do again. *Please, God, let her live*, he prayed.

"Yes, I do want to hear about you." Maybe it would help to keep her talking. Beckett realized he did want to know about Sadie, which came as a shock. On the streets, he kept his distance from other people. Handing out blankets was as close as he came to sharing genuine human connections. There was something significant about this event, however. Beckett got the feeling that Sadie was right about their meeting not being by chance. Had the woman in front of him not gotten belligerent with the transit officer, Beckett would surely have been thrown off the train. He'd wandered here, showing up to come to Sadie's aid.

His pulse increased when he saw headlights in the distance. "Someone's coming!" As carefully as he could, he extricated himself and placed her head gently on the ground. He ran over to the side of the road, waving his arms wildly. "Stop!" he yelled. His heart dropped when the car passed without stopping. However, when it got a few paces away, it came to a halt. He jogged over to the car where a man haltingly rolled down his window an inch.

"There's been an accident. A woman's hurt. Call 911!"

1

FOUR YEARS LATER ...

Hearing the howl of the snowstorm outside made Beckett grateful to be in the warm fire station with his fellow crew members, his second family comprising the PCFD Station 3 C. They'd been together for two years, longer than any other crew in Park City. Becoming a firefighter, being a member of this crew, brought Beckett back into the world of the living. He sank into the recliner and stretched his legs on the foot rest as he glanced at the football game playing on the TV.

Garrett Macey the fire captain was sitting in a nearby recliner. "The first snowstorm of the season," he observed, looking out the window at the large snowflakes coming down.

"Yep." Beckett let out a long sigh. "I wish I could say I was ready for it." His time living on the streets had left a bad taste in his mouth about winter. He hoped that would eventually fade with time. Before everything fell apart, Beckett used to live for the snow, spending many an afternoon at a ski resort, blitzing down the black diamond slopes.

"Ready or not, here it comes," Garrett chuckled.

Garrett was the oldest member of the crew and the driving force that kept them on task. About the only time Beckett saw him ruffled was when he discovered his wife was having an affair with her personal trainer. Garrett hit rock bottom during their divorce. Knowing precisely what it was like to have his world ripped apart, Beckett was happy to lend emotional support to Garrett during his difficult time. Like Beckett, Garrett had a daughter. Even though the transition was hard on Garrett, Beckett could tell he was doing well

He followed Garrett's vision, which settled on JFK a rover who took their fellow crew member Jak's place when he was off fighting wildfires. JFK was glued to his phone, texting. Seeing Garrett's displeased expression, Beckett grinned inwardly. JFK was about to get lambasted, and he didn't even know it.

Garrett slapped his hands together as he got up from his recliner. "What's our station rule during family time?"

It took less than half a second for the rest of the crew to jump on board. "No phones during family time," Tom said, leaning over and snatching the phone out of JFK's hand.

"It's my device, I'll do what I want with it." JFK reached for it, but Tom tossed it to Charlotte the toughest kid-sister the fire station could have. "Seriously? You guys need a hobby," JFK said like the whiny neighbor who never quite got the family jokes.

"This is our hobby." Charlotte threw the phone high in the air to Beckett, who sat at the end of the row of recliners.

Enjoying the lighthearted banter that was an integral part of station life, Beckett quipped, "'Twas a month before Christmas, all snowy and white ..." He handed the phone off to Nikola who took up the rhyme in his Serbian accent.

"...Family time came, not a phone was in sight." Nikola tossed the phone across the room, but a hand shot from behind the recliner and snatched it out of the air.

The crew turned to see a shaggy-faced man standing there, grinning. Jak, the missing member of the crew, the prodigal son, had returned home.

"Sorry, sir, the homeless shelter is down in Salt Lake," Tom said, his expression deadpan. "This is a fire station."

"Wait," Beckett teased. "Look under the beard. He's kind of familiar. Didn't he used to work here?"

Jak casually tossed the stolen phone into the garbage can. "A guy goes away to be a hero for a couple months and you forget all about him?"

JFK cast Jak a crusty look as he dug through the trash, muttering something about being mistreated.

The crew descended on Jak, giving him shakes and bumping shoulders. Charlotte, the little wisp that she was, measuring at least a foot shorter than any of them, wiggled in and gave him a squeeze. "Welcome home, bro. We've missed you."

JFK's phone chirped. He looked at it. "Finally, some civilized company. My wife's here, I'll be downstairs in the community room." He shot them all an exasperated look.

The crew settled back into their recliners. With Jak home and the visiting firefighter gone they were a family again.

Garrett released a sigh of contentment as he stretched out in his recliner and placed his hands behind his head. "That's more like it." He nodded to Jak. "How go the wildfires?"

Jak shrugged. "Still burning. Snow here, drought there. I got three days R and R, then a couple of weeks out there."

"Good," Beckett said, falling into the teasing manner of firefighters. "JFK's got his eye on your spot."

"That's right," Tom added. "Says he's going to bid it."

"It breaks up the crew, but man can he cook," Nikola said, licking his lips.

"He also has never been house-trained," said Jak. "So, have fun with him."

"House-trained?" Charlotte questioned with a snort. "That's money coming from Chewy the Wookie."

Man, it was good to have Jak back. JFK was a decent guy, but he wasn't part of the family. Beckett cast his eyes around the crew. He and Charlotte, the only female, were medics. Tom and Jak were rescue techs. Nikola was the engineer, and Garrett the captain.

"What's new?" Jak asked, doing a full body stretch as he plopped down in his recliner. "What did I miss?"

"I'm not sure we should trust him," Charlotte said with a raised eyebrow and a devious smile playing at her lips. "I'm still not convinced that's Jak. We might need to take that beard off his face to find out."

Jak shot her a playful, bring it on, smile.

"You're such a skeptic," Tom said, slowly coming out of his recliner. With a tiny dip of his head, he invited the rest of the group to join him. "Only one way to find out."

Beckett jumped from his seat and joined the others as they rushed Jak, piling onto his recliner in a massive heap, threatening to snap the heavy-duty chair in half.

Before any more thoughts of razors or forced shaving could manifest, the chime of the doorbell brought them all to a standstill.

"I got it," Jak said glibly from the bottom of the pile.

"Yeah right," said Charlotte, already up and running for the door. "You don't even work here."

Jak fought free and raced after her, but Nikola caught him by the foot. Garrett rushed into second place as Jak shook off Tom's hand. All six of them raced for the front door, reaching it within a second of each other.

A cold wind, laced with shimmering snowflakes, spiraled around a figure standing on their front mat. There stood in front of them a hunched over, tiny figure draped in a brown cape with cottony white hair puffing out the sides of the hood.

"Come in," Garrett said, reaching out his hand to the stranger.

The figure tilted up its tiny head to display the smiling eyes of a little, old woman. She took Garrett's hand and wobbled by him into the fire station.

She patted Garrett's arm as she passed him, smiling with a mischievous, yet kind tilt to her mouth. Charlotte helped the woman remove her cape. Without it, she looked even more feeble.

"What are you doing in the snow?" Nikola asked. "Come inside, sit by the fire."

The six of them accompanied her upstairs. Garrett pulled a chair closer to the fire for her. Tom produced a blanket. Wanting to make her as comfortable as possible, Beckett offered her some coffee or hot chocolate. He couldn't stand the thought of this poor woman being out in the cold.

"No, dearies." The woman pulled the blanket tight. "None of you remember me?" An enigmatic smile touched her lips. "That will change."

There was something mysterious about the woman. Beckett could tell from the reactions of the other crew members that they shared his assessment. All six of them studied the diminutive woman. Nikola, Tom, and Jak sat nearby on the flagstone hearth. Charlotte perched herself on the arm of the woman's chair, ready to offer any assistance she could.

The woman reached deep into the cavity of her cape. She wiggled her arm around for a few seconds before pulling out a small, enclosed cake tin embossed with green leaves and small, red berries. "I made you a fruitcake," she announced gleefully, as a cartoonish smile splashed across her face.

Beckett suppressed a smile when he saw the mortified look on Garrett's face. This time of the year, well-meaning townsfolk dropped off treats and baked goods by the truckloads, more than any of them could possibly eat in an entire year, much less the holidays. Garrett had made his distaste for any type of fruitcake loud and clear.

There was something magnetic about the woman. Beckett watched as she used her arthritic fingers to slowly crack open the tin, causing a stale, candied fruit smell to infiltrate and spread throughout the room.

"Garrett," the woman said, removing a long, dull knife from the inside pocket of her cape.

"How do you know my name?" Garrett asked.

The woman only smiled in response.

Garrett eyed the fruitcake. When Garrett gagged, Beckett couldn't help but laugh softly. How was he going to get out of this one diplomatically?

"Thank you so much," Garrett said to the woman, reaching for the tin. "I'll place it on the counter with the other treats and we'll eat your wonderful cake after dinner."

The old woman tsked her tongue at him as she motioned with her eyes to the open space on the flagstone hearth that Nikola had vacated. Garrett had no option but to sit next to the woman. He looked terribly uncomfortable like he was sitting on nails.

"Now, dearie," she said with kind eyes. "Or would you like me to call you Garrett?"

"Garrett's fine," he clipped.

"Garrett." She nodded. "Fine name for a fine man. You lead this crew so well, making sure everyone else's needs are met. That everyone's happy. You wish for their happiness?" she questioned with a wink.

"Yeah," he stuttered.

She nodded. "So do I." She slowly cut a piece of her fruitcake as she hummed a Christmas jingle.

Garrett turned green as she slowly scooped the cake up in her bony fingers and held it out to him. She continued, "And what about Garrett's happiness?" She looked up at the rest of the crew and said in a loud voice. "Does Garrett, your captain, deserve love by Christmas?"

Laughter rippled through the group. "Yep, Cap deserves all the love he can get," Jak drawled.

"Here, here," Tom said.

"I couldn't agree more," Beckett added with a cheeky grin. It was fun watching Garrett squirm. His face was flaming to the point where it was almost purple.

"Eat my cake," the woman said.

Garrett swallowed hard. "I can't," he uttered.

"Oh, go ahead and humor the woman," Beckett urged. "Eat the cake." He'd learned from sad experience that a person would eat nearly anything when hungry enough. Lucky for him, Garrett had never had to go through that, which made him a picky eater.

The woman muttered something about a girl named Maci and M&Ms. It seemed to rattle Garrett, although Beckett had no clue what she was talking about. He chalked it up to the ramblings of an old lady. How many times had Beckett seen people who were half out of their minds? Often, his time on the streets seemed like it happened in another lifetime. Having the old lady here brought it all back full force, making him extremely grateful for where his life was today.

Finally, Garrett closed his eyes and popped it into his mouth. Beckett and the other crew members waited for his reaction. Beckett half-expected him to spit it out, but instead, he opened his eyes and proclaimed in surprise, "It's really good."

"Of course it is, dearie," said the lady.

Garrett's expression changed as he tipped his head. "Did we?" he said, then stopped.

"Yes, dearie?" she questioned with encouragement.

"This may sound strange, but did we help you move into a white cottage home on Main Street last spring?" Garrett asked.

Yes! Now Beckett remembered. No wonder there was a sense of familiarity surrounding the woman. They had helped her move. She seemed eccentric, yet kind. The years seemed to peel away, and the lady suddenly looked a decade younger than she had a few moments ago.

She clapped her hands together, giggling in delight. "Yes! I knew you'd remember." She leaned close to Garrett, "Now go get your love before Christmas."

"Get my love?" Garrett asked dubiously.

"Go," the woman commanded, dismissing him as she summoned Tom to join her with a wave of her hand. One-by-one, she went through all of them, giving them a piece of the cake and muttering some nonsensical phrase. Soon, it was Beckett's turn. When he sat down beside her, she studied him with such intensity that he felt like she was burning a hole through him. "You've been through much hardship, have known the ravages of hunger, the emptiness of the streets." Her eyes took on a wise light. "You've had to battle the greatest demon of all ... the one that resides inside you."

A shiver ran through him. "H—how?" he blustered. Had someone told the lady about his past?

"You are on the right path, but forgiveness doesn't come easily. Nevertheless, your heart will guide you. Trust your feelings." She paused, gazing into his eyes. "God doesn't keep score of the miracles He gives you. It's okay to ask again."

He tensed. "What do you mean by that?"

She dismissed the question with a wave of her hand, a benevolent smile stretching over her lips. "You will find the love you seek by Christmas ... and something else."

The love he sought? He wasn't seeking love! He'd sworn off love a long time ago. The only love he felt was for Jasmine. Had someone put this lady up to coming here to toy with them? Beckett wasn't amused. In fact, he was fast becoming ticked.

She gave him a reproving look. "How quickly your temper rises. Your head has sworn off love, but your heart never will."

The woman had read his thoughts. He was dumbfounded, disturbed. "How are you doing this?"

Her eyes danced with mirth. "Just remember. All that glitters is not gold."

"Huh?" Okay, that made absolutely no sense. The woman was clearly crazy.

Charlotte grinned in amusement. "It's a line from Shakespeare."

The woman handed him the cake. "Eat," she commanded.

Mechanically, he placed it in his mouth and chewed. Garrett was right. It was delicious. The most delicious cake he'd ever eaten. A rush of something inexplicable went through Beckett, followed by tingles that zinged through his body like a cluster of shooting stars. He could've sworn he even heard chimes. There was definitely something unusual happening here. As he moved away from the woman, trying to make sense of it all, the firehouse bell rang through the building—car accident with injuries, extraction needed. The entire crew jumped from their positions of repose.

Garrett paused and Beckett could almost read his mind. He was concerned about the lady and what to do with her. They couldn't exactly throw her back out into the storm. She wouldn't last through the night in a storm like this.

Jak touched Garrett's arm, "Go ahead, Cap. I'll stick around until you get back."

Garrett gave Jak a hearty thanks.

As they hurried from the room, Beckett stole a glance at the tiny woman. She caught his eye and smiled. Again, he felt like she was seeing into some secret part of him. *All that glitters is not gold.* He had no idea what that meant, but felt sure it would somehow play a significant role in his life.

Two hours later, when they returned to the station, they found Jak sitting alone in the dayroom, staring into the fire. "The old lady. She's gone," Jak said, his eyes fixed on the motion of the amber flames. "I turned around to get her a drink of water, and when I looked back, she was gone."

"What do you mean, gone?" Garrett asked.

Beckett saw the concern in Garrett's eyes, knew that the safety of the crew and security of the station came down to him as a captain.

"Poof," Jak said. "Just without the noise. She gave me my ... fruitcake prophesy, just like she gave you, then she started coughing, so I got up to get her a glass of water. Then ... poof."

"Fruitcake prophesy?" Charlotte chuckled. "Is that what you're calling the crazy talk of a homeless person?"

Nikola pulled a face. "I have to agree with Charlotte. You're all acting a little strange after eating that fruitcake and I'm going to get to the bottom of this."

"Fruitcake prophesy?" JFK chimed in. "From a crazy homeless person?" He held his hands in the air, waiting for answers that didn't come. "Where was I?"

Beckett felt unsettled, concerned. The woman knew he'd had rough shakes. Had referenced his time on the streets. His past wasn't something that Beckett publicized. The crew knew about it, but few others did. Maybe he'd met the woman during his time on the streets, possibly given her a blanket.

"Let's look around," Garrett suggested, ignoring their commentary. "Make sure she didn't just go to another room and pass out or something." He put his arm around Beckett and asked in a low tone, "You okay?"

Beckett nodded, but he was rattled, and he knew it showed on his face. He tried to pinpoint what had him on edge—maybe fear that the woman wandered off into the night. Or, maybe it was because she seemed to know so much about his past.

Jak stood to join the manhunt. "That's a good idea, just so you guys can rest easy, but I already searched every inch of the station."

"We'll call it a night drill," Garrett said. "Nikola, JFK, Tom, and Beckett—primary search of the first floor. Charlotte, Tom, and I will do a primary search of the second floor. Then we'll switch and do a secondary search."

Garrett turned to Jak. "What's that famous gut of yours telling you about all of this?"

Beckett wasn't surprised that Garrett was asking Jak's opinion. When it came to fireground operations and rescues, Jak had terrific instincts. More times than not, his gut instinct was right on the money. Garrett and the rest of the crew had come to bank on it.

"It's legit," said Jak simply. He looked around, his eyes meeting everyone's in the group. "Hold onto your Santa hat, because things are about to change for all of us."

Even as Jak spoke the words, Beckett knew he was right.

Things were about to change.

CHAPTER 2

Beckett looked sideways at Jazzie and grinned a little at the stubborn tilt of her chin. The older Jazzie got, the more she was starting to take on his traits. Poor girl. He felt for her and the hard knocks she'd have to experience. She was eleven years old and already cocking an attitude. Heaven help him when she turned into a teenager. Hopefully, Beckett could help her navigate through the rough spots so she wouldn't make the same mistakes he'd made.

A stormy expression brooded over her face. "It's not funny, Dad. I hate Dave. He's not my father and has no right to tell me to eat my dinner or what time I need to go to bed." Her eyes narrowed. "That I can't use my phone when I want."

He let out a heavy sigh. "I totally get where you're coming from, honey, but Dave is your mother's husband. You need to show him some respect."

Jazzie folded her arms tightly over her chest. "Mom put you up to this, didn't she?" she asked accusingly.

Beckett held up his hands. "That's not important." Melinda had asked him to speak to Jazzie about Dave, but he wasn't about to admit it. He'd told Melinda that he'd see what he could do, but that he couldn't make any promises.

"Of course it's important," Jazzie exploded. "How can you sit there and act like it doesn't bother you that mom married another man?" Her voice trembled. "You should've fought for Mom. If you had, the two of you'd be together right now." Her features hardened. "And there would be no Dave to deal with."

He tried to figure out a way to make Jazzie understand the situation. "Your mom and I are in a good place. We both have your best interest at heart." Jazzie grunted and looked like she was about to say more, but he held up a hand. "Hear me out. I care about your mom. I always will." He paused, trying to figure out the best way to phrase the rest. "She seems happy with Dave. You should be happy for her."

Jazzie rolled her eyes. "Dave's an uptight moron who thinks everything has to be perfect all the time." She thrust out her lower lip. "You'd think we live in a museum. If one silly thing is out of place, he goes nuts."

"Really?" That sounded a little worrisome. Beckett wondered if he should talk to Melinda about that. He didn't want Jazzie having to walk on eggshells. Then again, maybe she was exaggerating. She was only eleven, after all. He made a mental note to keep his eye on the situation. He tried to stay out of Melinda and Dave's business as much as he could, but Jazzie's well being was his top priority.

Jazzie gave him a pleading look. "I just want me, you, and Mom to be a family again." She flicked her fingers on her jeans.

Tenderness welled in his chest. "Honey, we are a family. Me and you." Jazzie meant everything to him. He balled his hand into a fist. "We're as thick as thieves."

She lifted her chin, eyeing him. "And Mom?"

The last thing he wanted was to hurt Jazzie's feelings, but she needed to hear the truth. "I don't love your mother the way I did before ... when we were together. She's more of a friend or sister, both of us coming together with your best interest in mind."

Jazzie's eyes filled with dismay. "A friend? Sister? That's sick, Dad."

He chuckled. "No, it's just life." He blew out a long breath. "Look, Dave seems like a decent guy." He touched Jazzie's hair. "If you'll just be patient and give him a chance, I think you might be surprised at what can happen."

As she exhaled, he could see the wheels in her mind turning a mile a minute. "Okay, if Mom's out of the picture, then you need to find someone else."

He coughed. "What?"

"You heard me." A smile stole over her lips. "Come on, Dad. Even an ugly guy like you can find somebody. You have an okay personality, and you're semi-funny ... sometimes."

"Ouch," he countered, his lips turning down in a mock frown, "that hurt."

"Seriously, Dad. I don't like seeing you alone. You look so down-in-the-mouth all the time."

This time, he didn't have to fake the frown. "I'm not down-in-the-mouth." It hurt to know that Jazzie thought of him as sad or lonely. "I have a good life. I have you."

"I know, Dad," she said impatiently, "but it's not the same as having a girlfriend."

Had it really come to this—his daughter worrying about his love life? Or lack, thereof. He was pathetic. "Look, Jazzie, I know you're trying to help, but you don't need to worry about me finding a girlfriend."

"Dad, you just need to ask girls out. If you did you'd see—"

He cut her off. "It's not something that you need to be concerned about." The words came out harsher than he intended, and he cringed when he saw her wounded expression. Then her eyes narrowed as she shook her head, giving him a look of utter disgust that only a pre-teen could perfect. "You just don't get it, Dad." She opened the door of the pickup truck and got out, reaching for her bag. "See ya inside," she barked, slamming the door behind her.

He rubbed his jaw, wondering how the conversation had taken such a nosedive. What was in the water lately? First, the odd Fruit-cake Lady with her talk about finding love before Christmas and then Jazzie. It was like someone shook up a bag containing all his secret wishes and his number one desire ended up on top. Three weeks later, and he was still pondering over the Fruitcake Lady. A couple days after she showed up at the station, he went to the house he and his fire crew had helped her move into only to learn that another family lived there. They'd been there two years and had no knowledge of the little, old lady.

Beckett watched Jazzie walk across the parking lot. She was growing up fast, the awkwardness of childhood giving way to the bloom of femininity. Even though she was ticked, she was so nimble and light, every step filled with energy. Her limp was so slight that even he hardly noticed it. After dozens upon dozens of surgeries and more physical therapy than a person should be subjected to in a lifetime, she'd reached this point. Even the doctors were astounded at her progress, saying they'd never seen a recovery like hers, given the scope of her injury. Jazzie truly was a walking miracle. After coming off the streets, Beckett had prayed over and over that Jazzie would be healed. He wanted his little girl to live a normal life, not be punished because of his mistakes. He told God that if He'd grant him that one thing, he'd never ask for anything else. It was enough to have Jazzie whole. Several times, Beckett had been tempted to pray for more—to pray that he could find someone to love, to share his life with. Then, he'd remember his promise. He'd sunk so low and was given another chance. Jazzie had been healed. Truly, he was blessed. How could he ask for anything more?

Eventually, he swore off love, telling himself that he didn't need anyone. He was fine being alone—a sour grapes mentality. The Fruitcake Lady's words came rushing back about God not keeping score of miracles. Why did he keep thinking about the lady? How did she know that Beckett was afraid to ask for more? Was it okay to ask? The possibility was intriguing, a sliver of light falling underneath a closed door. *Love by Christmas.* He chuckled, rubbing his jaw. With Christmas a little more than two weeks away, it seemed like a long shot that he'd find anyone. It was for the best. He just needed to get that through his thick skull.

His thoughts went back to his conversation with Jazzie. Sure, it was hard seeing Melinda with another man, but mostly, Beckett was glad she'd found someone. He and Melinda's relationship was strained years before he even hit rock bottom and allowed the alcohol to consume him. Melinda craved a comfortable life with all the trappings of wealth, and Dave had given her that. A pediatric dentist, Dave had more money than he knew what to do with. He built Melinda a fifteen thousand square foot mansion in an exclusive, gated community nestled at the base of a canyon in Herriman. Melinda could now afford to buy expensive clothes, take trips whenever she wanted, and have lunch with her friends at nice restaurants. Dave gave Melinda everything she'd ever wanted. Kudos to him. As for Beckett, he was content with his job and salary. Sure he drove a used truck and budgeted his money, but a simple life was all he needed.

Beckett got out of the truck and reached for his bowling bag. Once a week, he drove down from Park City to South Jordan, a city near where Jazzie lived. The two of them had a standing bowling appointment. Also, a couple of Beckett's former neighbors and friends routinely joined them. He got a few steps away from the truck before he saw a young mother trying to open a baby stroller. A toddler stood beside her, and a baby was in a car seat on the ground. A second later, the toddler giggled and sprinted across the parking lot.

"Riley! Come back!" she yelled in exasperation, ready to take off after him.

"I'll get him," Beckett said, jogging across the parking lot after the toddler. The kid was fast widening the distance between them. Beckett sprinted, catching up to him about fifty yards from the main road.

"Woah, tiger," he said, grabbing the boy's hand and taking him back to his mother.

"Thank you," she breathed before giving the boy a reproving look. "Riley, you can't just run off like that." She took a firm hold on his hand, turning her attention to Beckett. "I got a new stroller and was trying to figure out how to open it," she explained. "Then Riley took off. I need more than two hands," she lamented.

Beckett looked at the round-faced baby in the car seat—another boy. "You've got your hands full."

She made a face. "Yeah, tell me about it. I'm meeting my husband here." She shook her head, letting out a heavy sigh. "Somehow, he thinks we're going to be able to bowl with these two."

"Here, let me see if I can help get that open for you." He placed his bag on the ground and reached for the stroller. After fiddling with it for a couple minutes, he figured out how to open it. He pointed to the red button on the side. "You have to press it hard to get it to open. If it continues to stick like that, you might want to take it back."

"Thank you." She gave him an appreciative smile. "Riley, hold onto the stroller," she instructed. Riley grabbed hold of the handle, swinging on it. The stroller tipped backwards. "Watch out." She righted the stroller, placing the car seat in it. Beckett feared he might have to run after Riley again, but luckily, he stayed put this time. Once the car seat was fastened in place, she caught hold of Riley's hand. "I really appreciate your help."

"Sure, I was glad to do it." They made small talk as they walked to the entrance of the bowling alley. When they passed through the double doors, the woman smiled. "Thanks again."

Beckett nodded. "You're welcome." It was such a little thing—taking the time to stop and lend a helping hand. Before his breakdown, he went full speed 24/7, never having the time or mindset to pay attention to others around him. Now, he made a point of not overloading himself with the superficial aspects of life, so he could be available to help when needed. Not that he was perfect at it, but he figured if he kept trying he'd keep walking in the right direction.

"Heya, Beckett," a peppy brunette with frizzy, gray-streaked hair chirped as she gave him a hearty wave.

"Hi, Annette. How's it going?"

"Oh, you know. Never a dull moment. I forgot to ask the last couple of times you've come in, but how was your Thanksgiving?"

"Good. Jazzie and I went to my parents' house. My brother and his family drove in from Colorado. It was good to see them. How about yours?"

"Fine. Can you believe it? Three weeks later, and we're still eating turkey. Charlie bought one of those fryers." She chuckled dryly. "He's been trying to fry everything that moves. I swear he even went after the cat the other day." She laughed at her own joke.

A grin tugged at Beckett's lips. Annette was a hoot. She and her husband Charlie a retired airplane mechanic ran the bowling alley. Just under five foot five inches tall, Annette was thin and wiry, but a pistol from the word *go*. Charlie was easy going, whereas Annette ran the bowling alley tight like a ship.

She gave the wad of gum in her mouth a good go-around as she flashed a wicked grin. "I hear Jazzie's gonna whoop you tonight, big guy."

He lifted an eyebrow, amused that Jazzie had been talking smack about him. "Is that so?"

"According to her. I told her I had to see that," she winked, patting his arm. Her face fell as she looked past him. "Hey," she yelled. "Stop throwing popcorn!" She pointed. "Yes, I'm talking to you clowns."

Beckett turned to see what all the fuss was about. Several teenage boys were in the chairs at the head of one of the lanes. Having been called on the carpet, they were frozen in mid-motion, sporting sheepish expressions.

"No more of those shenanigans or you're out of here!" Annette jerked her thumb towards the door.

"Sorry," one of the boys said dejectedly.

"Teenagers! They're gonna be the death of me," Annette muttered. "I think their parents just dropped them off here like we're some sort of babysitting service."

"I hear ya," Beckett chuckled.

Annette's face softened like fruit left too long on the counter. "Aw, now. You don't know. Jazzie's one of the good ones."

"Yeah, most of the time, when she's not trying to run my life."

Annette let out a throaty laugh that had the raspy sound of a smoker. "That's girls for ya." She frowned. "I'd better run and see why the lines are so long at the concession stand." She rolled her eyes. "Some of the workers take their sweet time. It's nearly impossible to get good help these days. See ya, Beckett." When she got a couple of steps away, she glanced back. "Oh, I'm looking forward to your little dance."

He waved a hand. "Yeah, yeah." Tradition had it that whichever one lost—him or Jazzie—had to do a dance to some outlandish, hokey song that Annette blasted over the speakers. The past three times Jazzie had lost, so she had to eat crow and do the dance. Tonight, Jazzie was out for blood.

Beckett strode over to the lane where Jazzie was waiting. As he sat down and removed his shoes, his phone buzzed. It was a text from J. C. saying he wasn't going to be able to make it tonight. "Well, J. C.'s out. Harry called earlier today and cancelled because his daughter had something going on at her school tonight. I guess that leaves you and me, kiddo."

Jazzie thrust out her lip in a pout. "Too bad. I was hoping they'd come."

"Me too."

Her eyes danced with laughter. "So, they could see you get your butt kicked by a girl." Jazzie rolled up her sleeves and went to retrieve her ball.

"You talk big for a little girl," he drawled, settling into his seat and stretching out his legs.

She just rolled her eyes. A second later, Beckett came out of his seat when Jazzie bowled a strike. Despite the friendly competition, he was fiercely proud of his daughter who excelled at everything she put her mind to.

Jazzie pumped a fist in the air. "That's what I'm talking about." She wiggled her eyebrows. "Your turn. Let's see you top that." She practically skipped to her seat.

Beckett stood and retrieved his ball. "You set the bar high." He held up the ball, eyeing the pins, before drawing his arm back and releasing the ball. At first, it went straight down the center. Then, at the last minute, it curved to the left, only hitting two pins. "Hey, there must be something wrong with that ball," he complained in jest.

"Or your aim. Too bad," Jazzie said in a singsong voice. She grinned. "I'm sure looking forward to your dance."

A smile stole over his lips. "Don't count your chickens before they hatch." This time, he corrected his swing, sending the ball right down the center where it landed him a spare. He pumped a fist, shooting Jazzie a triumphant look.

"Good recovery," Jazzie said admiringly.

As Beckett sat down in his seat, his eye caught on the woman bowling next to them. His heart skipped a beat. To say she was beautiful was as much of an understatement as saying Park City had snow in winter. The woman was stunning. Medium height, she was thin but shapely in tight-fitting jeans and a denim button-down shirt. Her long, honey-blonde hair bounced lightly against her slender shoulders as she moved. He knew he shouldn't stare, but he couldn't seem to take his eyes off her. She retrieved a ball from the return and walked to her lane, holding the ball to her chest. When she let go, the ball bounced noisily on the wood floor before toppling into the gutter.

Her shoulders dropped a fraction in disappointment as she went back to get her ball. She appeared to be alone. *Interesting.* It wasn't often that people bowled alone. He watched as she tried again. Like the first time, the ball went straight into the gutter.

As she walked regally back to get her ball, she must've felt Beckett watching her because she looked in his direction. Electricity jolted through him like a live wire when their eyes met. A stupid grin washed over his face, and he felt like he was sixteen again.

She smiled. It was a glorious, full-mouth smile that crinkled her eyes. Beckett couldn't tell from this distance what color her eyes were, but he was dying to know.

"Did you see that? Another strike! Two in a row," Jazzie announced, her voice singing with excitement.

The woman looked down as she reached for her ball, breaking eye contact.

"You didn't even see it, did you?"

"Huh?" He shook his head, coming out of the daze as he focused on Jazzie whose brows were scrunched, her face squished with irritation. She waved a hand in front of his face. "Earth to Dad. I just bowled another strike."

He forced his mind back to Jazzie. "Wow! Two in a row. You're on a roll."

"Yeah." She shot her fist in the air.

As Beckett stood, he couldn't help but steal another glance at the woman. This go-around, she managed to knock over three pins. Jazzie followed his eyes. A second later, her face lit up like a Christmas tree as she smiled broadly. "Ah, I see why you were preoccupied... because of her."

Heat blasted Beckett as he rubbed a hand over his neck. "No, that's not why. I got a text and was reading it," he fudged.

Jazzie folded her arms over her chest. "Liar, liar pants on fire." She looked at the woman, frowning. "One thing's for sure, she's a lousy bowler."

"Shh," Beckett warned. "She'll hear you."

Jazzie's eyes swirled with amusement. "You like her."

"That's ridiculous," Beckett scoffed, reaching for his ball, "I don't even know her."

A mischievous light flickered in Jazzie's dark eyes. "Well, let's see if we can do something about that."

Before Beckett could stop her, she jumped up and went over to the blonde. Beckett's face burned as he watched them talk. Jazzie said something and pointed to him. The woman smiled. Beckett was itching to know what they were saying. Then again, maybe it was better if he didn't know. Suddenly, he realized he was standing there like an idiot, holding the ball. He forced his feet to the alley, keenly aware that the woman and Jazzie were both watching him. *Focus!* He drew back and let the ball go. To his horror, it went straight into the gutter. Beckett couldn't remember the last time he'd bowled a gutter ball. *Sheesh!* How humiliating.

Jazzie's laughter floated over to him, but he willed himself to look straight ahead as he went to get his ball. This time, he was determined to redeem himself.

Using as much force and precision as he could muster under the pressure, he released the ball. He held his breath, watching as it barreled towards the pins, straight down the center. To his dismay, all the pins except for the ones on each end fell. It was a split.

The temptation was too great. He glanced at Jazzie and the blonde as he walked back to his seat. The woman flashed another brilliant smile that did strange things to his insides. A moment later, Jazzie came back bringing the woman with her! Beckett's pulse pounded like a fist against his ribs, his palms going sweaty. Normally, he was perfectly fine around the opposite sex. He didn't know why he was getting so bent-out-of-shape over this woman.

"Dad, I hope you don't mind," Jazzie began, "but I asked Ava to join us. Her friends didn't show up. It's no fun bowling alone."

Ava. A dignified, sophisticated name. It fit her. Up close, she was even more dazzling with bright blue eyes, perfectly proportioned features, high cheekbones and neat rows of white teeth. An easy smile slid over her dainty lips, revealing deep dimples in her cheeks.

She extended her hand. "Thanks for letting me join you."

Her voice was cultured with a slight lilt. He reached for her hand. A tingle went through him when their skin connected. Her hand was small and delicate enfolded in his large, calloused hand. When he held onto Ava's hand a second longer than necessary, Jazzie sniggered.

"Let go, Dad."

Immediately, he dropped Ava's hand as if it were a hot coal, making the situation even more awkward. Okay, maybe he was a little out of practice when it came to women. He felt like a bumbling buffoon. And, Jazzie wasn't helping. It registered in his mind that Ava was looking at him expectantly, as if waiting for him to respond. His name! He was supposed to tell her his name. Somehow he found his voice. "I'm Beckett." The words got caught in his throat as he coughed. "Sorry." He swallowed. "I'm Beckett," he repeated with more authority.

"Nice to meet you, Beckett." A gentle amusement sparkled in her eyes. They were a light, silvery blue, the color of the summer sky.

He loved how his name sounded on her tongue.

Ava glanced back. "Oops, I guess I should've gotten my ball."

"I'll get it," Jazzie said, being Little Miss Helpful.

Now that they were alone, Beckett wasn't sure what to say. "I haven't seen you here before. Do you bowl often?"

She laughed lightly. "I'm sure you can guess the answer to that question after seeing me bowl."

A smile twitched at the corners of his lips. "Yeah, that was pretty bad."

Her mouth fell. "Hey."

He held up a hand. "No offense. You saw my gutter ball."

"Yeah, but at least you didn't do two in a row."

He motioned. "Have a seat."

"Thanks." They both sat down. Gracefully, she crossed her legs and wrapped her hands around her knee. "In answer to your question, no, I don't bowl often. I was supposed to meet one of my clients and her kids tonight, but my client cancelled at the last minute." She shrugged. "I was already here when I got her text, so I figured, *What the heck!* I'd give it a try."

"I'm glad you did." For an instant, he feared that he was coming on too strong, but her radiant smile put him at ease.

"Me too."

Their eyes locked as attraction stirred inside him. The connection between them was electric.

Jazzie returned with the ball and placed it on the return. She sat down in front of the digital pad that controlled the score. "Let's add you to the game."

Annette strolled up to their table, eyeing Ava. "Are you joining Beckett and Jazzie?"

"Yes," Ava answered.

"It's a packed house. We've got people waiting. Do you care if I give your lane to someone else?"

"No, not at all."

Annette's eyes sparkled as she gave Beckett a sly look. "You kids have fun," she chirped.

"Thanks," Beckett said pleasantly, ignoring Annette's inference.

Jazzie looked at Ava. "All right. Got you in the system. It's your turn."

Ava grimaced. "You saw how terrible I am." She laughed self-consciously, running her slender fingers absently through her long tresses of gold.

"My dad can teach you the basics," Jazzie said slyly.

Beckett wanted to put a muzzle on the little stinker. Jazzie was about as subtle as a moose.

"Would you mind?" Ava asked.

No doubt Ava could tell that Jazzie was throwing the two of them together, but she didn't seem bothered. "Sure," he found himself saying.

They stood, and she went over and picked up her ball. Anticipation buzzed through his veins at the thought of being so close to Ava. *Hold it together, man.* The key was to act nonchalant, like being next to an exquisitely gorgeous woman was the most natural thing on the planet. He stood behind her and placed his arms over hers. Her arms were sinewy and defined, making him wonder if she worked out. As he leaned in, her hair tickled his nose, and he caught a whiff of her fruity shampoo mingled with the light floral scent of her perfume.

He cleared his head, willing himself to concentrate on the task at hand. "Be sure and keep your wrist straight when you draw back. As you come forward, rotate your hand toward the opposite side of your body. When you release the ball, your hand should be in the handshake position with the thumb up."

"What?" She shook her head. "That's too much to remember all at once."

"Okay, start with focusing on keeping your hand straight and then go from there."

"I can't."

"Sure, you can." She smelled so wonderful. He closed his eyes, breathing her in.

She chuckled lightly. "Not until you release my arms and stand back."

He felt foolish. "Oh, sorry." He stepped back a few paces. "All right. You've got this." He used his hands as he spoke. "All right, draw back. Wrist straight. Let it go. Now!" His voice raised. "Follow it through. Arm goes to the opposite leg, around your ankle."

The ball dropped with a heavy thud against the wood as Ava let out a disappointed yelp. The ball rolled at a snail's pace three-quarters of the way down the lane before falling into the gutter. She squeezed her hands into fists. "Dang it!"

"It's all right. You'll get the hang of it." He thought of something. "How much does your ball weigh?"

"Eight pounds."

"Ah." He touched his forehead. "Makes sense. It's too heavy for you. Let's try a six-pound ball."

She wrinkled her nose. "I tried to find one earlier, but couldn't."

"You can use Jazzie's ball."

Ava went to the return and reached for Jazzie's pink ball. "Do you mind if I use yours?"

Jazzie waved a hand. "Sure, go for it."

Ava put her fingers in the ball and tried again. This time, the ball rolled more smoothly onto the floor, but still went into the gutter.

She held up her hands. "I'm a lost cause."

"Nope," Beckett countered, "you'll get the hang of it."

She chuckled. "Well, I can't get any worse."

Next, it was Jazzie's turn. She hit seven pins down the first try and got the other three on the second attempt. Ava clapped as Beckett hooted. "Way to go, Jazz!"

This time around, Beckett got a strike. "Yes!" His eyes found Ava's as she smiled. In that moment, Beckett felt like he was the king of the room. The very air tingled with excitement now that Ava was here.

Ava took her turn. This time, she managed to knock down six pins on two tries. As she strode back, she shrugged. "Better, right?"

Beckett grinned. "Yep, much better. We'll make a bowler out of you yet." Beckett was surprised and pleased when Ava sat down beside him. A part of him wished they weren't at the bowling alley. He wanted to be alone with Ava so he could find out more about her. When Jazzie got up to take her turn, he angled toward Ava, intent on getting in as many questions as he could during the short few minutes they had before Jazzie returned. "You mentioned that your client couldn't make it tonight. What type of work do you do?"

"I'm a freelance interior designer."

"Wow, that's awesome. I'll bet it's a fun job."

She tilted her head, her brows drawing together in thought. "Most of the time." She tucked her hair behind her ear. Her gold hoop earring shimmered as it caught the light. "It's like anything, I suppose. It depends on the project. How about you? What do you do?"

"I'm a fireman."

"Impressive," she murmured. Her light eyes moved over him with admiration. "I should've known. Take-charge attitude, those tough-guy muscles, the confident swagger in your step."

He was taken back by her forthrightness. As juvenile as it was, he was flattered that she'd noticed his muscles. "Thanks," he chuckled softly.

"I knew you were one of the good guys when I saw you in the parking lot, helping that lady with her stroller."

His eyes rounded. "You saw that?"

Ava smiled brightly. "Yep." She held up a finger. "But don't let it go to your head."

"I wouldn't dream of it."

Ava pointed. "Jazzie just got another spare. The pressure's on."

"Take that, Dad," Jazzie taunted with a smile the size of Texas plastered over her face.

Beckett stood. "All right. Here we go." He felt light enough to fly as he went to the foul line and bowled. After all was said and done, he left two pins standing. When he went back to the table, Jazzie shook her head. "I can't wait for the dance."

"Dance?" Ava asked dubiously.

In an animated fashion, Jazzie told her all about the dance. Ava grinned at Beckett. "I'm so glad I came here tonight. This is gonna be fun."

"Yep, sure is," Jazzie agreed.

The corners of his lips pulled down. "Hey, no fair—the two of you ganging up on me."

As Ava took her turn, Jazzie turned to him, a crafty look in her eyes. "You like her, a lot."

He thought about denying it, but knew Jazzie could see right through him. "Yeah, a little, I suppose." He couldn't stop the grin from pulling at his lips.

"I like her too," Jazzie said in a matter-of-fact tone, like she was pronouncing judgment. "You'll be happy to know that I looked at her ring finger. No wedding ring."

A shiver ran through Beckett, followed by a swift rush of relief. He should've checked, but he'd been too mesmerized by Ava to think about it. Thank goodness, she wasn't married! That would've been disastrous.

Jazzie's voice grew excited. "Look, Dad. There's one pin left. She might get a spare." Beckett looked at the single pin standing in the center of the lane. Ava looked back at him for reassurance, her expression hopeful.

"You can do it!" He held his breath as she drew back and released the ball. Slowly, it rumbled towards the pin like it was going in slow motion.

"Come on," Jazzie said. "Go!"

The ball touched rather than hit the pin. It wobbled slightly, then finally fell.

Ava jumped up and down. "I did it!"

Without thinking, Beckett was on his feet, rushing towards her. He caught her in a hug, doing a victory dance with her. "That was awesome!"

She beamed up at him. "Thanks! I owe it all to you."

Awareness tingled through him, and he realized he was still holding her arms. Awkwardly, he let her go. *Sheesh!* Things were moving fast, maybe too fast. *Don't overthink it,* his mind warned as they went back and sat down.

When the game was over, Jazzie held up her hands and hopped around. "Told you I'd win tonight," she said enthusiastically.

Beckett made a flourish with his hand. "I take off my hat to the winner. Great game, honey."

Jazzie embraced him in a hug. "Thanks, Dad." She pulled away, her eyes sparkling. "All right, you know what comes next." She looked towards the bowling shoe counter where Annette was standing. "Do you see that score?" She pointed to the screen, flashing her name as the winner.

"Yep, sure do," Annette said loudly. "Good game, Jazzie!"

"It's time," Jazzie said.

Beckett grimaced as he got to his feet. Normally, he didn't mind doing the dance, but tonight in front of Ava he felt a little timid about it. The "loser" song blared over the speakers as all eyes in the bowling alley turned to watch Beckett. At this point, there was only one thing he could do—ham it up. He started dancing and singing his heart out like he was a superstar. About midway through, everyone began clapping to the beat of the song. When the dance was over, ripples of applause sounded around the room. Beckett gave a low bow. He knew his cheeks were red when he went back to Jazzie and Ava.

Jazzie grinned, showing her braces. He looked at Ava to get her reaction. When she smiled, warmth blazed through him.

"Not bad for a hero fireman," she murmured, her eyes holding his.

Later, after everything had settled down he would ponder over Ava's use of the word *hero*. Here and now, he felt like the luckiest guy in the world. He'd gone to his usual haunt to bowl with his daughter, only to discover an unexpected prize along the way. For some strange reason, the prize seemed to be as taken with him as he was with her.

"Thank you. That was fun." Ava removed her bowling shoes.

Beckett's stomach clutched. He didn't want this evening to end, not without getting Ava's number. Even as he was trying to broach the topic without sounding desperate, Jazzie blurted out, "Tomorrow night, Dad and I are going to my grandmother's house to decorate Christmas cookies. Would you like to join us?"

The startled look on Ava's face jolted Beckett. Maybe he'd misread the situation. His heart fell though this ribcage and rolled onto the floor like Ava's bowling ball had done. He gave Ava an apologetic look, then aimed his words at Jazzie. "Honey, Ava doesn't wanna do that." Maybe it was all just a fleeting dream. Yeah, he was a sap. No one fell in love at first sight. That was something for the movies and romance books. True life was much stickier.

"How do you know?" Jazzie countered, her chin drawing into her neck like a turtle. "You haven't even given her a chance to answer."

Beckett wanted to crawl under the industrial carpet beneath his feet. "I'm sorry," he said to Ava. "We didn't mean to put you on the spot." He forced a smile.

"You didn't," Ava said simply. She gave him a wounded look, her eyes holding his. "You don't want me to come?"

He stuttered out a nervous laugh. "Of course, I want you to come. I just didn't want to assume ..." His words trailed off when he realized he didn't know how to finish the sentence. Assume what? That Ava would want to spend more time with him? That this overwhelming connection was a two-way street? He knew his face red.

Ribbons of amusement streaked through Ava's light eyes. She knew how intensely uncomfortable he was right now. "I'd be honored to come."

"You would?" Beckett croaked.

"Yes." Ava smiled at Jazzie. "Thanks for inviting me."

Beckett's insides did a victory dance. *Ava was coming tomorrow night!* It was like he had to keep repeating it to make himself believe it. He could've hugged Jazzie for being so precocious and for butting into his business. "Let me put your address and phone number into my phone, and I'll pick you up tomorrow night."

"No need," Ava said quickly. "I have a meeting scheduled in the late afternoon with a client. I'll just meet you guys there."

"All right." Beckett was a little disappointed. He would've loved to have seen where Ava lived. Would loved to have ridden with her alone so they could talk. Then again, beggars couldn't be choosers. It was enough that Ava was going.

Love by Christmas. Suddenly, it didn't seem like such a far-fetched idea, after all.

CHAPTER 3

Ava brushed away the thick layer of snow and placed her hand on the tombstone, the cold from the marble seeping through her gloves and up her arm. The impersonal words block-printed across the front made it all too real. *Milton McQueen*, his birthdate and death date summing up the whole of her grandfather's life. It was still hard to believe that her grandfather was no longer here. He was larger-than-life, her anchor. A lump formed in her throat, tears filling her eyes. The ground was still soft and squishy from the burial. Her eye caught on the wilted red roses, stiff with snow, the tips blackening with decay.

"Hey, Granddad. I told you I'd come and visit." She laughed to clear the pain. "You'll be happy to know that I actually met Beckett. He's everything you always said and more. No, I didn't tell him who I am." She fought off a shiver. "That will come soon enough."

An image of Beckett flashed through her mind. His deep brown eyes that were lively one minute, compassionate the next. His chiseled jaw with just the right amount of scruff. His lean muscles and the fluid way he moved. How he wore his masculinity casually like a second skin. His easy manner. The way he'd made her feel so alive when he'd stood behind her, teaching her how to bowl. Beckett was a poster boy for every girl's dream of a hunky firefighter—tough enough to fight fires, yet considerate enough to stop and help a struggling mother with her stroller and young toddler. The friendly neighborhood Spiderman and Superman melded together. She pushed back a lock of hair, swallowing. Yeah, she wasn't about to say all those things out loud. This wasn't about her silly infatuation with Beckett Bradshaw. This was about a promise that she'd made to her grandfather. One she was determined to keep. "The plan is in place, just as we discussed." Her voice cracked. "In fact, I'm meeting Beckett tonight to decorate cookies." She frowned. "Don't judge me, please. I just want to get to know him, find out what sort of man he really is. You know, before ..."

For the past two weeks, she'd tried to decide if she should approach Beckett or just let the natural order of events progress. She'd gone to the bowling alley, not intending to have any personal contact with him. At the last minute, she decided to bowl rather than just lurking in the shadows. As luck would have it, she was assigned the lane next to Beckett and Jazzie. She'd not thought twice about it at first because only Jazzie was there. When Beckett came in, Ava freaked. Her plan was to bowl a couple of frames and then leave before drawing attention to herself. However, Beckett noticed her right off the bat. When she felt Beckett's eyes on her, all reasonable thought flew out the window and like an idiot, she found herself basking in his admiration. Then, Jazzie came over and asked her to join them. At that point, what could she do?

Last night was the first time since her grandfather passed that Ava felt a part of things. She'd enjoyed the easy banter that passed between Beckett and Jazzie. How they included her in the conversation. The mere thought of being around Beckett again thrilled her to the core. She pulled her coat tighter around her and glanced around at the deserted cemetery. How silly she must look out here, talking to a tombstone. Her granddad wasn't here. She didn't know where he was, exactly. Heaven, hopefully. He wasn't in the cold, hard ground though. That knowledge had been instilled in her during the funeral and burial. Still, she needed a place to go, somewhere to feel close to him.

A black wall of hurt rose, threatening to crumble over her as a sob clogged her throat. "I miss you so much." Loneliness engulfed her like a giant fist, squeezing her insides so that it was hard to breathe. She let out a bitter half-laugh, her breath freezing the moment it left her mouth. "Ted and Libby are furious, just as you said they would be. You were smart to add the no contest clause. Hopefully, it will keep them at bay."

She paused, tears dribbling down her cheeks. "If you can hear me..." Her lower lip trembled. "Please know that I love you." She smiled tightly, taking in a shallow breath. "That's all for now."

She wiped her eyes and turned, averting her face from the wind as she walked briskly back to her car, the tips of her stilettos digging into the snow-covered ground with every step.

Ava pulled alongside the curb in the middle-class neighborhood, checking the address on the house against the one on her GPS. This was the right place. She turned off the engine and took in a deep breath, trying to calm the jitters in her stomach. *Just breathe.* Beckett's pickup truck was here. Having personal contact with Beckett probably wasn't the smartest move, but she couldn't seem to help herself. All day long, she'd been looking forward to this. When Beckett realized who she was and what part she'd soon play in his life, how would he react? Would he be hurt, thinking that she'd deceived him? Or would he understand that she just wanted to find out more about him before everything changed.

She got out of the car and straightened her shoulders, willing her feet to move towards the door. Her phone rang. She reached in her purse and pulled it out, frowning when she saw who was calling. Wesley. He was the last person she wanted to speak to right now. She clicked the button on the side to silence the ringing and shoved the phone back into her purse. A second later it buzzed, signaling that

Wesley had left a message. She sighed. How many times did she have to keep telling him it was over before he'd get the hint?

When Wesley proposed, she turned him down as diplomatically as she could. Then, he insisted she keep the ring and think about it. A week later, she told him she had thought about it and that her answer was still *no*. A couple days later, Ava's grandfather passed away. Wesley had been wonderful, offering a listening ear. Ava had no one, other than her grandfather's attorney Houston who wasn't much for conversation. In her weakness, she'd poured out her heart to Wesley. Unfortunately, he took that as a sign that the two of them were back together. Ava would, *again*, need to tell him that they weren't a couple. Wesley probably thought he could wear her down, but that wasn't going to happen. Not in this lifetime.

Approaching the door, she pushed the doorbell. Jazzie answered it with a broad smile. "Hey, I'm glad you came." She waved. "Come on in."

"Thanks."

"Ava's here," Jazzie announced loudly as she bounded out of the foyer and through the adjacent living room, leaving Ava no other choice but to follow. The Christmas tree in the left corner had festive red plaid ribbons, various ornaments mostly made of wood, and blinking colored lights. The fireplace next to it was adorned with greenery and stockings. The right side of the living room opened to a large kitchen. When Beckett saw her, a warm smile overtook his rugged features as he strode over.

"Hey," he said as they hugged.

Feeling his strong arms, Ava was unprepared for the rush of tingles that circled down her spine. He smelled fresh and clean, distinctly masculine. Also, there was a hint of the sweet aromatic scent of baking cookies. Ava looked past Beckett to the woman standing beside the kitchen island. She bore a strong resemblance to Beckett, or vice versa. Candy cane earrings dangled beneath her short, dark hair streaked with brilliant red highlights. Her sparkling eyes were dark like Beckett's with an intelligent light glimmering in them. Tall and thin, she was very attractive. No doubt she'd been a knockout beauty in her younger years.

The woman offered a welcoming smile. "Hello," she said, wiping her hands on her Christmas apron.

Beckett made introductions. "Mom, this is Ava. Ava, this is my mom Harmony."

Harmony extended her hand. "It's nice to meet you."

Ava gave it a firm shake. "Nice to meet you too. Thanks for having me. You have a lovely home. And Christmas tree."

"Thank you," Harmony said appreciatively. She tipped her lips in the same crooked smile Ava had seen Beckett give the night before. "My husband Phillip keeps telling me that I need to scale down, now that the children are grown and out of the house, but I can't imagine Christmas without our family decorations."

"Tell Granddad you do it for the grandkids," Jazzie chirped, reaching for an undecorated cookie and biting a large hunk out of it.

"That's right," Beckett interjected heartily, smiling affectionately at Jazzie. "Dad might as well get used to the decorations. They're here to stay."

"My sentiments exactly," Harmony agreed, her chin squaring with determination. "I wish Phillip was here so you could meet him. He's out visiting with some members of our church congregation tonight."

"I'd like to meet him sometime," Ava said.

"Next time," Harmony smiled.

"Here, let me take your coat." Beckett stepped behind Ava and helped her remove it. The close contact sent her pulse hopping. Beckett also took her purse. "I'll put these in the living room." He walked over and deposited her things on the sofa.

Ava's eyes did a quick sweep, noting how nicely his broad shoulders filled out his shirt. She trailed down to his tapered waist and long, jean-clad legs. *Sheesh.* Even the way Beckett walked was attractive. His steps were light and jaunty. He was super fit like he could take off running this minute and do a marathon with little effort. Heat blotched up her neck when she realized Beckett's mom was watching her watch him. *Awkward!* She flashed Harmony an apologetic look, but Harmony only smiled like it was no big deal, the slightest hint of amusement lighting her eyes. Harmony was probably used to women admiring Beckett. How could they not? He exuded such charisma and masculinity that he must draw women to him like the Pied Piper. The thoughts of other women fawning over Beckett sent jealous darts shooting through her. Ava laughed inwardly, thinking how ridiculous this inner dialogue was. She had no right to be jealous about Beckett. They hardly knew each other.

Ava's mind raced, trying to come up with something halfway intelligent to say. She'd wanted to come here so badly. Now that she was here, however, she felt awkward and stiff. She walked over to the cookies, examining the various shapes and sizes. They were all so perfect that they looked like they'd come from a bakery.

Jazzie motioned. "Choose which one you want to decorate."

"Maybe I should wash my hands first," Ava said.

"Sure, go right ahead." Harmony pointed to the nearby sink.

Her hands washed and dried, Ava was ready. She felt like a kid as she looked at the decorating bags filled with red, green, and white icing. Also, there was a large assortment of sprinkles. She selected a Christmas tree, figuring that wouldn't be terribly difficult. Then again, she had little experience decorating cookies. Time would tell. She pulled out a barstool and sat down. Warmth sparked through her when Beckett sat down right next to her, so close their knees were nearly touching. He reached for a cookie shaped like a candy cane. Ava assumed he planned to decorate it. Instead, he took a giant bite. "Um, that's good," he murmured.

"Hey, now," Harmony scolded. "We need to at least decorate a few cookies before you guys gobble them up." She frowned, looking back and forth between Beckett and Jazzie.

"I like 'em better without frosting," Beckett said with a shrug.

Jazzie made a face. "I like both." She paused. "Maybe the iced ones better."

Harmony held up a finger. "I promised the committee ladies at church that I'd donate ten dozen for the cookie exchange."

Ava went bug-eyed. Ten dozen? Wow, that was a lot of cookies. Harmony was a saint.

A grin slid over Beckett's face as if reading Ava's mind. "The minute Thanksgiving's over, Mom starts baking and doesn't stop until New Year's. She won't rest until she's given cookies to three quarters of the population in Park City."

"Probably more than that," Jazzie piped in.

"That's not true," Harmony blustered, lightly slapping Beckett's arm.

"It's true," Jazzie mouthed, then clamped her lips together, her eyes laughing, when Harmony gave her a sharp look.

Harmony let out a long sigh, her hand going to her hip. "As you can see, my family gets great delight out of tormenting me." Her expression was solemn, but there was a hint of amusement in her eyes.

"We love you, Mom," Beckett said soothingly. "We're glad you like to bake." He touched his flat stomach. "I'm only complaining because if I hang around here too long, I won't be able to fit into my pants."

"Oh, stop." Harmony shook her head. "Men," she muttered, giving Ava a conspiratorial grin.

Ava laughed, her tension dissolving. She picked up the green icing and piped it over the cookie. After it was base coated, she made red balls for ornaments. She attempted to do a red bow for the top, but it looked pathetic. Beckett and Jazzie also went to work, decorating their cookies. A few minutes later, when the cookies were complete, they inspected them. Ava's wasn't great, but the sprinkles helped make it look decent. Jazzie's Santa was cute, but simple. Ava's jaw dropped when she saw Beckett's snowman. It was pristine, every detail artfully done. He even added in the plaid on the scarf.

"How," she sputtered, "did you do that?"

Jazzie made a face. "Show-off," she pouted.

Harmony looked at it, flashing Beckett a doting smile. "Yep, you're still the master."

Beckett reddened a little under the praise. "Ah, it's nothing," he said nonchalantly.

"You may not know this about Beckett, but he's an artist," Harmony explained, pride sounding in her voice.

"Really?" The rough and tumble firefighter was also an artist? Ava shook her head. "No, I didn't know that." The more she learned about Beckett, the more surprises there were. He was a fascinatingly complicated man.

Jazzie laughed in amusement. "How could Ava know? She and Dad only met last night."

Harmony looked surprised. "Oh, I didn't realize. The two of you seem so well suited for each other."

Well suited for each other. Ava liked the sound of that.

Beckett's mouth moved like he was trying to figure out how to respond. Before he could, Jazzie chimed in, her tone matter-of-fact. "Yeah, we were at the bowling alley. Ava was in the lane next to us, and Dad couldn't stop making googly eyes, so I asked her to join us."

Harmony laughed in surprise. Beckett's face turned tomato red and he made a gurgling sound like a sock was stuck in his windpipe. So, he'd been checking her out. Ava thought—*hoped*—that was the case. He was so darn cute that Ava couldn't help but laugh. Beckett gave Jazzie an exasperated look. "Do you have to tell everything?"

Jazzie grinned like a Cheshire Cat. "Well, it's true." She shrugged. "Ava must like you too, Dad, or she wouldn't have come here tonight." She looked at Ava expectantly. "Isn't that right?"

All eyes flew to Ava as she coughed. *Dang it!* Now a sock was stuck in her windpipe. She knew her face was flaming like a beacon. Now would be the appropriate time to utter a cute quip to downplay the situation, but no words would come. She felt like everyone could see right through her, and they would know she'd longed to get to know Beckett for some time now.

"I'm sorry," Beckett began. He shot Jazzie a reproving look. "There are times when it's wise to use discretion."

Jazzie wrinkled her nose. "What's discretion?"

"Never mind." Beckett laughed, shaking his head. His eyes held Ava's. "You'll never want to come here again."

"No," she blurted, "that's not true. I'm enjoying every minute of being here." She smiled at Jazzie. "I'm glad you invited me to join you last night. I can't remember when I last had such a good time."

Beckett cocked his head, a pleased smile tugging at his lips. "Really?"

"Really," Ava said softly, thinking how she could get lost in the depth of his rich liquid-brown eyes. It wasn't fair for a guy to be so good looking, not pretty but rugged and chiseled. A man's man. Her gaze took in his lean jaw, firm lips. Heat simmered in her stomach as she wondered how his lips would feel against hers.

"That's good," Beckett uttered softly.

Harmony cleared her throat, her eyes sparkling. "Uh, let's get back to decorating cookies."

Ava jerked, her skin burning with the heat of embarrassment. What was it about Beckett that had her so enthralled? She couldn't remember the last time she'd felt so alive, like a new world of opportunity had unfolded. A part of her wished they could just stay like this, two people who met spontaneously and fell in love. She jerked inwardly, hardly believing she'd thought such a thing. *Love? Really?* She was losing it, for sure.

"I can show you a few decorating techniques," Beckett offered.

"Sure, that'd be great." A smile quivered at her lips.

"What?" he asked, giving her a quizzical look.

She gave in to the smile as it filled her face. "I just have a hard time reconciling the firefighter with the cookie decorator."

Beckett's face fell as Harmony's warm laughter filled the room. "Maybe we should call you Beckett Crocker."

"Seriously?" Beckett complained.

Harmony's lips drew together sheepishly. "Sorry. Bad joke."

Jazzie hooted. "If your crew heard about you decorating cookies, they'd never let you hear the end of it."

"That's why they don't need to ever hear about it," Beckett said firmly, but Jazzie only laughed.

"Wait until I tell Captain Garrett and Char! She'd love to hear this."

Beckett shook his head, grinning. "Garrett and Charlotte are members of my firefighter crew. And you're right. I'd never hear the end of it if they found out." He gave Jazzie a beseeching look. "You wouldn't oust your old man, would ya, princess?"

Jazzie sighed, twisting a finger around her curl. "I guess not."

Everyone laughed.

Harmony brought her hands together. "All right. Get to work. I'd like to have these decorated before next Christmas."

"She's such a taskmaster," Beckett lamented, tsking his tongue.

"There'll be hot chocolate afterwards," Harmony added, "with marshmallows."

"Yes!" Jazzie said.

"Dangling that carrot, huh, Mom?" Beckett teased.

Harmony grunted. "I have to dangle something for you to get to work." She reached for the snowman and placed it on a separate plate. "I'll just put this one aside for the cookie exchange." She motioned. "Go ahead, Son, work your magic. The ladies at the church are counting on you."

Beckett made a face. "Now you know the real reason she wants us to decorate cookies. Free labor."

"That's right. Get to work," Harmony said, winking. "Chop, chop."

He chuckled, letting out a long, labored sigh. "All right, Mom. Just know that I only do this for you. 'Beckett Crocker'," he muttered under his breath. "I still can't believe you said that." He chose another cookie and went to work decorating. Ava did the same. Jazzie, however, slid off the stool.

Beckett's brows drew together. "Hey, where're you going?"

Jazzie thrust out her lower lip, folding her arms over her chest. "I'm tired of decorating. I'm going to watch a movie." Jazzie gave Harmony a pleading look. "May I, please?"

"Of course," Harmony nodded.

The corners of Beckett's lips turned down in a mock frown. "I see how it is," he joked. "You let the princess go relax while the slave works."

Harmony just laughed as Jazzie slipped out of the kitchen.

CHAPTER 4

When it was just the three of them, Harmony looked at Ava. "So, tell me about yourself."

Glancing at Beckett, Ava could tell he was keenly interested in what she had to say. She gathered her thoughts, trying to decide how much she should tell them. "I'm an interior designer." It was always good to start with the career, that was neutral enough.

"Oh, no." Harmony's eyes rounded as she glanced around the kitchen. "Now, I'm embarrassed for you to see my house. There's so much that needs to be done."

"Your house is beautiful," Ava countered, "truly. I love the homey feel."

Harmony's face brightened. "Thank you." She looked thoughtful. "I want to redo Phillip's study. Maybe you could give me some tips."

"Sure, I'll be happy to."

"I can pay you."

Ava waved a hand. "No need for that," she said quickly. "Let me just help as a friend."

Harmony's eyes clouded. "I don't want to take advantage—"

"You won't, I promise," Ava assured her.

"Thank you," Harmony said.

"You're welcome." Ava could've lived a month on the look of appreciation Beckett gave her. Her insides turned to mush as she smiled back. Not wanting another embarrassing moment with the two of them gazing into each other's eyes, while Harmony looked on, Ava looked down breaking the connection. A beat of silence stretched between them, and Ava realized they were waiting for her to tell them more about herself. She wet her lips. "I grew up in Biloxi, Mississippi."

Beckett tipped his head. "Really? You don't have a Southern accent."

"No, not anymore. I used to. My mom died when I was sixteen, so I went to live with my dad and grandparents."

"I'm sorry," Harmony said.

"Thanks," Ava responded casually. "It was a long time ago." Truthfully, going to live with her dad and grandparents had been the best thing that ever happened to Ava. Before that, life was hard.

"Where do your dad and grandparents live?" Harmony asked.

Ava's throat tightened. "They're all gone."

Beckett looked up, frowning. "Gone?"

She forced a smile. "Yeah, my dad died when I was eighteen. He had a congenital heart defect. No one realized until it was too late." The sympathy on their faces evoked a wave of emotion. Ava blinked rapidly. Her sorrow wasn't for her dad. She'd long since made peace with his death. It was her grandfather's death that had punched a hole in her heart. Mechanically, she answered the question she knew they were probably thinking. "I don't have the defect. My grandfather had me tested." The relief on Beckett's face was surprising and flattering. Maybe he was starting to care a little about her too. She rushed to finish the rest. "My grandmother died a couple years ago. And, my grandfather..." Tears misted her eyes. She swallowed, looking down. Beckett touched her hand. His touch was both comforting and thrilling. A tear escaped the corner of her eye. She laughed, brushing it away with her free hand. "I'm sorry."

"No need to apologize," Beckett said.

"Thanks," she uttered, laughing humorlessly. "Normally, I'm not this emotional. It's just that my grandfather passed away two weeks ago. I'm still trying to deal with it."

"I'm so sorry." Harmony gave her a concerned look.

"That must've been rough." The tenderness in Beckett's tone seeped into her heart. Their eyes connected. In them, she saw a depth of feeling of one who'd also known pain and heartache. Gently, he squeezed her hand.

"Yes, it was." All she could think about was his hand over hers, the warmth of his long, tapered fingers.

Harmony's features tightened with concern. "Do you have any family left?"

The words rushed out. "My aunt, uncle, and their kids. But we're not close." *Not close?* She chuckled darkly inside. That was the understatement of the century. Ted and Libby hated her guts, almost as much as they'd hate Beckett when they found out what was coming down the pipe.

Why in the heck was she telling Beckett and Harmony all this? To make them feel sorry for her? She was pitiful. She drew in a breath. "I'm sorry. You don't want to hear all this."

Beckett removed his hand, and she immediately felt the loss of his closeness.

"Yes, we do," Beckett argued. A look passed between Beckett and Harmony.

"What?" Ava asked, feeling as though she were missing something.

"We want you to spend Christmas with us," Harmony said.

Ava's eyes rounded. "Huh?" She looked at Beckett who was studying her intensely. She moistened her lips, her throat going dry. "Um, I don't want to intrude."

"You don't want to have Christmas with us?" Beckett asked, a challenging look in his eyes.

Ava smiled. This was reminiscent of her response the night before when Jazzie invited her to decorate cookies. "Of course, I want to. I just don't want to impose."

The idea of spending Christmas with Beckett and his family was glorious. Then again, everything would change soon and they may not want her spending Christmas with them. Suddenly, she wondered if her grandfather's plan was flawed. Beckett and his family were happy as they were. Maybe it was wrong to mess with their lives. Too late now. Everything was in place. Irrevocable. No turning back, not even for Ava. Her grandfather had made sure of that.

Harmony brought her hands together, smiling broadly. "Good, it's settled. You'll spend Christmas with us."

"Don't think that gets you off the hook," Beckett added.

She rocked back. "Huh?"

A crooked smile stole over his lips. "I plan on the two of us spending lots of time together."

The sure promise in his voice made her insides purr. "I'd like that," she heard herself say.

After the cookies were decorated and they drank hot chocolate, it was time for Ava to go. "Thanks again," she said to Harmony who gave her a tight hug.

"Come back soon."

"I will," Ava assured her. Beckett's mom was the picture of class, yet down-to-earth, the kind of person Ava could see herself being friends with. *Hopefully, I'll still be welcome after everything goes down.*

Ava picked up her coat and purse, waving to Jazzie who was kicked back on the recliner, a large bowl of popcorn in her lap. "See you later."

"Bye, Ava. Thanks for coming." She flashed Beckett a wicked grin. "I'm sure we'll be seeing you again."

"Yes, we will." His gaze lingered on Ava long enough for the intimate smile in his warm eyes to stoke a flame inside Ava's heart.

Jazzie's face twisted in disgust. "Yuck, Dad. Get a room."

Beckett jerked, his head whirling around to Jazzie. "Excuse me?"

"Sorry," Jazzie squeaked, her cheeks turning pink.

"That's not acceptable," he said, his tone unyielding.

Jazzie looked down at the popcorn bowl, her expression turning glum. "I said I'm sorry," she muttered. "*Geez*, why're you making such a big deal about it?" She stirred a finger through the popcorn.

"Because it is a big deal." Beckett turned to Ava. "I'm so sorry."

She smiled, feeling sorry for Jazzie. "It's okay." She leaned close to Beckett and whispered. "She probably just heard that somewhere and doesn't even realize what it means."

He rubbed his neck. "Yeah, I suppose so." He paused, looking at Jazzie. "I'm walking Ava out."

Jazzie nodded, her eyes on the TV like she was glued to it, so she wouldn't have to engage with Beckett.

Beckett helped Ava put on her coat and placed his hand on the small of her back as they went to the door. When they stepped outside, a blast of wind hit them full force, snowflakes swirling. Ava shivered, hugging her arms. "You shouldn't be out here without a coat."

"I'll be fine," Beckett said offhandedly. "I'm used to the cold." He walked her to her BMW Wagon. Briefly, Ava wondered what Beckett would think of her high-priced car, but he didn't seem bothered by it in the slightest. His focus was one-hundred-percent on her.

"Thanks for coming tonight." He stepped closer, sending a thrill shooting through her veins. "I'd like to see you again."

The question shot out of her mouth like a rocket. "When?" She winced. *Sheesh*. That sounded forward.

Beckett laughed. "How about tomorrow?"

Ava felt like she was cresting the incline of a rollercoaster, about to rush headfirst on the greatest thrill ride of her life. "I'd like that."

He placed his arms around her, pulling her close. "There, that's better. You can keep me warm."

"Wait a minute." She pulled back and opened her coat, attempting to put the sides of it around Beckett. He slid his arms around her waist. Anticipation danced out a wild beat against her chest. Was this really happening? She lifted her face to his, drinking in the exhilaration of his nearness. In the shadow of the street lamp, the outline of his jaw resembled granite. Tonight, he was more Superman than Spiderman—all grown up and larger-than-life. She parted her lips expectantly, welcoming his touch. His jaw brushed against hers, his stubble tickling her skin with a tantalizing persuasion. Passion swirled around Ava, engulfing her in a heady cloud as their lips began a sensuous dance of give and take. Her insides melted with pleasure as she reveled in his closeness.

All too soon, Beckett pulled away. Ava could tell he'd held back. She appreciated his reserve, knew it was the right thing. Still, she craved more of him. She wanted to run her fingers through his messy hair, explore the defined muscles in his back. She wanted to kiss him with reckless abandon until there was nothing left in the world but the two of them.

He motioned with his head. "We've got an audience."

Ava looked toward the front window. The blinds moved slightly. "Jazzie?" Color rushed to her cheeks. She couldn't help but chuckle. "She's something."

"Yep, she's something, all right," he responded dryly. He flashed a hopeful smile. "Tomorrow, then?"

"Yes," she said exuberantly. "Where should we meet?"

The corners of his lips turned down. "I was thinking I could pick you up."

He couldn't know where she lived. Not yet. She laughed lightly. "I have a few client meetings scheduled. One at eleven. Another at four. I'll be out and about. I can meet you somewhere around six. How does that sound?" She knew how rushed her words sounded, feared he could see right through her and would know she was hiding something.

He masked his disappointment with a smile. "Sure. I suppose I've gotten spoiled with my work schedule. Forty-eight hours on and four days off. I forget that everyone else works five days a week."

"Yeah, most of the time I can be flexible, since I work for myself. It's just when I have set appointments ..." Her voice trailed off.

"I understand."

"What're we doing tomorrow?"

His eyes glittered. "It's a surprise."

"A surprise, huh? I like surprises."

She loved how his gaze moved over her face, like he was memorizing every detail. "I had fun tonight."

"Me too."

"Until tomorrow then."

She touched his cheek, her fingers lingering on the firm plane of his jaw. "I'll text you when I'm done and we can decide where to meet."

He helped her into her car and closed the door. As she drove away, she glanced in the rearview mirror, hardly believing that they'd actually kissed! She touched her lips, still feeling the burn of his on hers. She could only imagine what her grandfather would say if he could see her right now. The thought sent misgivings rushing through her. She'd not meant to get close to Beckett, yet she wanted this. These feelings ... they were more than mere infatuation. The Beckett of her daydreams had been replaced by the living, breathing version who was a thousand times more awesome than she could've ever imagined.

"Until tomorrow," she said aloud as she headed for home.

Conflicting feelings warred in Beckett's gut as he watched Ava drive away. On the one hand, he was riding high from the kiss. *Wow!* She'd lit a fire in him that left him wanting more. She was an angel—intoxicating. Not only was she incredibly beautiful, but more importantly, she seemed like a good person. She'd fit in well with his mom and Jazzie. Apprehension tugged at him. On the other hand, he got the distinct feeling that Ava was hiding something. Last night at the bowling alley, she said she'd just meet him here to make cookies. He was disappointed but didn't think too much of it. He and Ava had just met. He figured she was being cautious, not jumping into a vehicle with a guy she barely knew. Tonight when he offered to pick her up, she'd danced around the topic again. He could feel her nervousness, knew there was something she wasn't telling him. Why didn't she want him to go to her home? A chill ran through him. Was she married? Surely not! His heart pounded out a sickly beat against his ribcage as he balled his fists. This was ridiculous! Getting so worked up over the hypothetical. Ava seemed like a good person. He could feel that about her. He needed to hold to that feeling. He dismissed the misgivings, refusing to let his fears get the best of him.

Every time something good happened in his life, Beckett grew uneasy, wondering when the other shoe would drop. He glanced towards the front window. Yes, Jazzie was spying on them, the little stinker! However, that wasn't the only reason Beckett held back. The truth was—he was afraid to embark on another relationship. What if the pressure became too great, like it had before? He couldn't go down that dark path again. It would destroy him.

Of course, that was different. It had been the combination of his high-stress work environment and failing marriage that drove him to drink. Still. He wasn't sure if he was up for another relationship. Maybe he'd never be ready. *Coward!* his mind screamed. Hadn't he just thought yesterday how he wanted to find someone? The Fruitcake Lady's words came rushing back. She'd said he would find love by Christmas. Was that what this was? The beginnings of love? Christmas was two weeks and one day away.

As he turned back toward the house, a prayer rose in his chest. He didn't pray to find love. No, despite what the Fruitcake Lady said about God not keeping score, he didn't feel like he could pray for that. Rather, he prayed for clarity to make sense of his feelings. He was grateful for the sense of peace that immediately came, wrapping him like a warm blanket. This thing with Ava. It was a good thing. He could feel it. He squared his jaw, resolving to hold onto the feelings of calm and keep moving in the right direction.

Tomorrow, he'd go out with Ava again, see how things went. Even as the thoughts flitted through his mind, an unexpected feeling of certainty flooded through him. Whatever Ava was hiding, she was still good. He could feel it, knew it as well as he knew his own breathing.

Things would go well with Ava. Even though they'd just met and were starting their relationship, it was real. More real and lasting than anything he'd ever known before.

As he stepped inside, Jazzie was waiting for him, an impish grin on her lips. "It went well, huh?"

He laughed and tousled her hair. "Yes, very well." He shot her a reproving look, a note of tenderness coming into his voice. "You wretched, little spy."

"Who me?" she asked innocently. "I didn't see a thing." Her eyes radiated laughter as she made a smooching motion with her lips.

"Uh, huh," he countered, ruffling her hair.

She drew back. "Hey, you're frizzing my curls," she protested, scrunching her nose.

He laughed. "Come on. Let's go help clean up the mess from the cookies."

Her face caved. "Do we have to?"

"Yes, we do," he laughed, putting his arm around her shoulders as they walked towards the kitchen.

CHAPTER 5

When Ava pulled up to the private drive leading to the mansion, she pressed in the familiar code as the gates swung open. She jerked as she drove through, realizing another car had pulled in behind her, close on her tail. Who could be coming to the mansion this time of the night? Ted or Libby? She tightened her grip on the steering wheel, hoping she wouldn't have to deal with either of them tonight.

Ever since her grandfather passed, Ted and Libby had been breathing down her and Houston's necks, demanding to know the terms of their father's will. Surprise, surprise. There was no will, but a living trust, which would keep everything private and succinct. Houston, her grandfather's attorney, met with Ted and Libby at 2 p.m. earlier today to discuss the terms of their personal inheritances. Had he also gone over the no contest clause surrounding the living trust? All day long, Ava had expected to receive angry phone calls from Ted and Libby. Surprisingly, however, no calls had come. Maybe that's because they wanted to attack her in person.

She glanced in the rearview mirror. The headlights were glaring. From her vantage point, it seemed like they were inches from her bumper. She flipped her rearview mirror up so the blinding lights wouldn't be directly in her eyes. The farther she got down the long drive, the madder she became. Ted and Libby got a decent inheritance, the same amount as Ava. Why couldn't they be satisfied with that? Ted still had his CEO position at the company where he was paid a salary close to 500K a year and that didn't include his bonuses. Libby's husband Bill was the CFO of the company. He was also paid very well. They were all vultures with an insatiable appetite for money, which is why her grandfather refused to leave any of them his trust. He wanted it to go to someone who was responsible, someone who would look past his own needs and wants to see the value of others.

The mansion came into view. She pulled into the driveway, following it alongside the mansion to the back of the seven-car garage where she hit the clicker and opened the door on the far left, driving in. She left the garage door open as she got out of her car and strode around the back of it, preparing herself for battle.

She frowned when she realized who was coming towards her. "Wesley? What're you doing here?"

"Hey, Ava." He touched her arm. "I called you a few times, but you didn't answer."

She ignored the accusation in his voice, discreetly pulling her arm away.

"Where've you been?"

She didn't appreciate the possessiveness of his tone. Straightening to her full height, she looked him in the eye. "That's none of your business."

He rocked back, his jaw going slack. "I'm sorry, I don't mean to pry. I was just worried about you." The overhead lights reflected off his blonde hair and handsome face, emphasizing the concern etched over his features. A year ago when Wesley first came to work for her grandfather's company as the marketing director, Ava was enamored by his stunning good looks and charm. As the two of them got to know each other, however, she realized that there was no spark. All Wesley would ever be to her was a friend. In contrast to Beckett, he seemed soft and over-polished; his movie-star looks a little too much for her taste. A Harvard Business School graduate, Wesley had been recruited by her grandfather and relocated to Salt Lake City from New York. A genius at marketing, Wesley had been a huge help to the company and a close friend of her grandfather's.

She relaxed, letting out a breath. "No, I'm the one who's sorry. I didn't mean to jump down your throat. It's been a long day." A long, wonderful day with Beckett. Maybe that was part of the reason she was disgruntled that Wesley was here. Before seeing the headlights, she'd been wrapped in the thrilling memory of Beckett's kiss. Now, she was back down to earth, dealing with the fallout from her grand-father's death. And, Wesley's over-protective tendencies.

He gave her a searching look. "I've missed you."

The whiny edge in his voice had the same effect on her as a fingernail scratching down metal. "Wesley." A nervous laugh escaped her throat. *Geez.* She didn't want to do this tonight, but there seemed to be no way around it.

"You look beautiful," he blurted, "as always."

His puppy-dog expression made Ava feel sick. She didn't want to hurt Wesley, but there seemed to be no way around it. She never should've let her guard down and cried on his shoulder. She should've been strong, held her ground.

Wesley suppressed a shiver. "It's cold out here. Mind if I come in?" His eyes smiled. "We can make some hot chocolate, watch a movie."

"I don't think that's a good idea. I'm tired."

"All right. I'll come back tomorrow morning, take you to that French café you love downtown."

She pulled her coat tighter around her, searching for the right words to let him down easy. "Wesley, please know that I appreciate everything you've done for me, especially during the funeral."

"Of course." An adoring smile glowed on his face. "You know I'd do anything for you."

"You've been a wonderful friend." She forced out the rest. "But, friends are all we'll ever be."

His face fell. "After everything we've been through together, I thought—"

"I know, and I'm sorry." The words fell out between them like heavy bricks. She took in a breath. "I didn't mean to give you the wrong impression."

He shook his head. "Don't do this, Ava. I know you love me. You just need time to figure things out."

A humorless laugh rattled her throat. There was no easy way, better to just come out with it. "No, Wesley, I don't need time. As much as I hate to say it, I am not in love with you. All the two of us will ever be is friends." How many times did she have to repeat the same phrase for him to finally understand?

His expression hardened. "This is about that firefighter, isn't it?"

She jerked, her stomach dropping. "What?"

"I saw you with him tonight, kissing him," he uttered in disgust.

Shivers went down Ava's spine. She clenched her jaw. "Were you spying on me?"

He barked out a laugh. "No, I wasn't spying. I was checking on you. There's a difference." His voice hardened. "Let's go in and talk about this."

No way was she letting Wesley into her house. From here on out, it was doubtful that the two of them could even be friends. She glanced around, realizing she was out here alone with Wesley. Bridgett and Mac, the couple who oversaw the mansion, were probably asleep by now.

"There's nothing to talk about," she heaved through clenched teeth. "You had no right to follow me."

He sneered. "You and some fireman? Get real." His voice grew musing. "Is this the one that your grandfather was fascinated with? The one who saved the kid from the fire? Milton followed his life for some time." He gave her a checkmate look. "Didn't think I knew about that little pet project, huh?"

"It's late, and I'm tired." Her voice sounded as weary as she felt.

He caught hold of her arm. "Ava! I won't let that guy come between us!"

An incredulous laugh rose in her throat. "When are you gonna get it through your thick head? There is no *us*, Wesley!"

"You're confused, letting your grandfather's fancies color your judgement." He tightened his hold on her arm, his fingers digging into her flesh. For a wiry, thin guy, he was surprisingly strong.

The hair on the back of her neck rose. There was no one to come to her rescue. "Let go of my arm," she demanded, her voice rising.

Wesley's eyes narrowed to black slits. For a second, Ava thought he might refuse, but finally, he released her arms and held up his hands. "You're making a big mistake," he seethed.

She bristled, her anger giving her courage. "Is that a threat?"

He looked at her for one long, agonizing moment before he spoke. "No," he said sadly, his shoulders sagging. "I would never threaten you. I love you." A regretful smile stretched over his lips. "I'm just sorry you don't feel the same way."

"Me too." She meant it with all her heart.

"I guess that's that, huh?"

The finality of his tone brought with it a swift rush of relief. "Yes," she said softly.

He touched her cheek, his eyes going soft. "Good night, Ava."

She fought the urge to draw back from his touch. "Good night."

He turned on his heel and walked briskly to his car, driving off.

Ava hurried inside. She didn't let out a breath until the garage door was closed and she was safely inside the mansion. Her mind whirled. The exchange with Wesley was odd. He knew about Beckett. Then again, in a few days, it wouldn't matter what Wesley knew. Her thoughts went back to Wesley's behavior. One minute, he was angry and belligerent. The next, he was wounded, placating. Did she need to be worried for her safety? Wesley had followed her, watched her and Beckett kiss. A shiver ran down her spine as she hugged her arms. She felt so violated. Her heart lurched. Was that how Beckett would feel when he learned the truth?

Without warning, tears sprang to her eyes. Oh, how she missed her grandfather. She wished he was here to help guide her through all that was coming. Hastily, she swiped the tears away with her palms as she trudged up the curved staircase to her bedroom, wanting nothing more than to snuggle in her bed and get a good night's sleep.

As Beckett walked past the food booths at the Christmas festival, he caught a whiff of cinnamon and cloves, mingled with the fresh scent of spiced apple cider. The aroma of baking bread enveloped his senses, causing his mouth to water. Were he not supposed to meet Ava by the large Christmas tree in five minutes, he might've been tempted to stop and purchase a loaf.

He wove his way through the crowd of people toward the center area and tree. His eye caught on the white lights of the tree at the same time he heard singing from the choir. He stood, watching the performance as he waited for Ava to arrive. Ten minutes later, she still wasn't here. He pulled out his phone to see if she'd sent him a text. Nothing. Apprehension snaked down his spine. Was Ava standing him up? He'd thought of little else other than Ava since last night, looking forward to the moment when they'd meet. He sent her a text.

Hey, I'm at the festival by the tree. Are you still coming? I hope everything is okay.

It was a clear night, but bone cold. Maybe this wasn't such a great idea, after all. Ava probably hated the cold. Last night, she seemed to have had a great time. He saw the longing on her face when he ended the kiss prematurely, felt her excitement over meeting him tonight. Or, maybe not. Was it possible that he'd misread the signs?

Even beneath his gloves, Beckett's fingers felt stiff from the cold. He shoved them in his coat pockets, his good mood dissolving. Coming to the festival alone was no fun. He'd hang out another fifteen minutes or so and call it a night. Disappointment cut through him like a dull knife, causing his insides to ache. His relationship with Ava had ended as quickly as it began. He was surprised by the feeling of loss that engulfed him.

A second later, adrenaline spiked through Beckett when he spotted Ava coming toward him, looking festive in a crimson coat, her blonde hair flowing gold tresses over her shoulders. When she saw him, an unencumbered smile curved her lips, revealing adorable dimples. That one simple expression smoothed his ruffled feathers, and everything was good again.

He closed the distance between them, pulling her into a tight hug, inhaling the berry scent of her shampoo. "Hey, you look fantastic."

"Thanks," she murmured appreciatively. "I'm so sorry I'm late. My client meeting went over. Rugs that have been on backorder for three months finally arrived. What was supposed to be a burnt rust turned out to be cranberry." She grimaced. "My client was not happy, especially considering she's throwing a Christmas party tomorrow night, and the rugs were going in her living room."

"What did you do?"

"I went to a local rug shop and rounded up a couple of replacement rugs. We're shipping the other ones back for a full refund." She waved a hand. "Anyway, it took longer than I thought to get here with traffic." She wrinkled her nose. "Parking is crazy here."

He laughed, feeling deliriously happy. "Yes, it is. I was worried, so I texted you to make sure you were okay."

Her eyes rounded. "Oh, I'm sorry. I didn't even realize."

"No worries."

She glanced around. "This looks fantastic. I've heard about it for years, but never had the chance to come."

He liked the idea of introducing her to something new. "Until now," he said significantly, his eyes holding hers.

Her light eyes sparkled. "Yes, until now."

He reached for her hand and squeezed it, appreciating how small her hand felt in his. "What do you want to do first?"

She looked at the choir. "Let's listen to a few more songs." She tipped her head. "Do you mind?"

"Not at all. When we're done with this, I'll show you the booths. Are you hungry?"

A full smile broke over her face. "Starved."

"Good. Me too. We'll grab a snack here, and then go to dinner." He pumped his eyebrows. "After we visit the booths, I've got a surprise for you."

She laughed. "I thought the festival was the surprise."

"Part one."

"Hmm." She pursed her lips, giving him an admiring look. "One thing I'm learning about you is that you keep me on my toes."

"Absolutely," he responded heartily.

She removed her hand and threaded her arm through his, leaning in close. "We'll help each other stay warm."

That's all the prodding Beckett needed to pull his arm away from hers and, instead, slide it around her shoulders, drawing her close. "How's that?"

"Much better," she said as she reached up and linked her gloved fingers through his.

There was so much Beckett wanted to know about Ava's life and past. He wanted to get to know every detail about Ava: how she chose her career, her hobbies, and favorite foods. Now wasn't the time to bombard her with questions. It was enough to just have her here with him.

As the choir sang *Joy to the World*, Beckett had the feeling that, for the first time in a long time, he was experiencing joy. Before his mind was even conscious of what was happening, his heart offered a prayer of gratitude for this moment, being with such an exquisite woman who seemed to like him as much as he did her. Yes, it was a joyful night. Hopefully, a sign of many more to come.

CHAPTER 6

"Are we going ice skating?" A surprised laugh rose in Ava's throat as she turned to Beckett. After listening to the choir sing, they toured the booths, purchasing hot chocolate and a loaf of some of the most delicious bread Ava had ever eaten. Then, Beckett told her it was time for the second part of the date. She never expected him to lead her to an outdoor ice skating rink.

A wide smile stretched like warm taffy over his lips. "Yep," he said proudly, his dark eyes lit with adventure. "Now comes the all-important question."

"Oh, yeah. What's that?"

"Can you skate?"

"Pshh," she uttered dryly, waving a hand. "Can I skate? Of course, I can skate." She paused, giving him a sheepish look. "A little," she admitted. "Truthfully, I'm not that great at it." She figured she'd might as well come clean now. In a few minutes, Beckett would see how terrible she was. She'd only been skating twice in her lifetime—when she was a teenager—and those were miserable failures. Still, with Beckett at her side, she was willing to give it a shot. Her brows drew together. "I didn't realize this rink was here."

"It's a new addition to the festival," Beckett explained. His dark eyes radiated confidence. "Don't worry. I'll stay right by your side, and I will be there to catch you if you fall."

"Famous last words," she chuckled. "I'll fall and take you with me. We'll both need knee replacements by the end of the night."

"Nah, we can do it. You'll see."

After they'd gotten their skates and put their things in a locker, they walked across the rubber mat leading to the ice. Ava's stomach squeezed as she tightened her grip on Beckett's arm. "This could end badly," she muttered.

"You'll be okay," Beckett countered. "Trust me."

Trust me. It was astounding how those two little words settled so comfortably into her heart. She did trust Beckett, more than he realized. He was so handsome in his manly, rugged way. It wasn't just Beckett's looks and charisma that drew her in, however. It was his strong, noble character that had caught her grandfather's attention and then, in turn, made her take note of him. Gradually, the admiration turned to infatuation. Now, that she'd met Beckett, she realized that her feelings for him were developing at warp speed. He was everything she'd ever hoped and infinitely more. She smiled to herself as she glanced at the determined set of Beckett's jaw as he led her out onto the ice. He was so capable and determined.

They skated a couple of feet forward. Then it happened! Panic raced through Ava as her feet slid out from under her. Her arms flailed as she tried to catch her balance. Beckett caught her around the waist, righting her, before she toppled backwards.

She turned to face him, clutching his coat, her feet going back and forth across the ice in a frantic attempt to gain traction.

"Take it easy," he said calmly. She felt his warm breath on her face as his eyes locked with hers. "I've got ya. Now, I'm going to turn you around and skate behind you, holding your waist."

She hiccuped a laugh. "All right." She swallowed, steeling her resolve as he turned her around.

"Lead with the right foot," he said in her ear. "Smooth, easy strokes."

How in the world was she supposed to concentrate on skating

when he was this close? All she could think about was the tickle of his breath against her ear, his strong arms around her waist.

He uttered a low chuckle. "No panicking. Let the skates guide you. The blades will cut into the ice, holding you up."

"That's easy for you to say," she countered. She forced her mind away from the powerful attraction she had to Beckett and looked at the ice before them. Kids were skating effortlessly as easy as walking. She could do this! She took in a breath. "All right." She went forward, repeating Beckett's instructions in her mind. *Smooth, easy strokes. Let the blades cut into the ice.* A couple minutes later, exultation swept through her. She was skating! The ice felt smooth, her skates moving swiftly through it. She concentrated on the steady motion, grateful Beckett was behind her, holding her waist.

When they'd made a full circle around the rink, Beckett moved to her side and took her hand. She felt a twinge of alarm, realizing his arms weren't around her anymore. She squeezed his hand for all it was worth.

He laughed. "You've got a grip like the jaws of life."

She lifted her chin. "Yeah, because you're my lifeline."

"All right. You're getting the hang of it."

After the third time around the rink, Ava was starting to feel better about the situation. The movement of skating was more liberating than she could've imagined. The cold kissed her nose and cheeks, making her feel exquisitely alive. She glanced at Beckett, who flashed her a pleased smile. "You're doing it."

"Thanks to your help."

"Would you like to try it alone?"

"No!" she sputtered at the same instant he released her hand. Her heart did a few flips as she continued. She leaned too far forward and almost fell, but managed to stand up straight. Everything clicked, and she was sailing!

She might've been okay, had the kid not stopped three feet in front of her. Her eyes widened as she tried to move around him to avoid plowing him over. Right before she hit the boy, Beckett grabbed her waist as they both toppled to the ground. Ava sat up in a daze.

Beckett got to his feet and helped her up. "You okay?"

"Yes." Amazingly, she was perfectly fine. Her jeans were slightly wet, but that was all. "Are you okay?"

"Yep. I'm great." He made a face. "I guess I shouldn't have promised that we wouldn't fall, huh?"

She smiled. "You didn't. Only that you'd be there to catch me if I fell."

He pulled a face. "I somewhat caught you, or you caught me. I'm not sure which." His eyes lit with amusement.

"Yeah, me neither. I warned you that I'd fall and take you with me," she teased.

"I'll take a fall with you anytime," he declared.

They stood, facing one another, Beckett's arms around her waist. Despite the cold, Ava's heart beamed sunshine as she studied his handsome face, his brow touched with the wisdom of one who'd suffered much and survived to tell the tale. He was strong-minded and steadfast. This, combined with his depth of compassion and understanding of the complexities of life, made him irresistible. Awareness rippled through her as she looked at his firm lips, longing to kiss him again. His eyes darkened with intensity. "Ava, I think I'm falling for you," he whispered before his warm lips came down on hers. The kiss sang through her veins as their lips moved together slowly, deliberately. The only thing that made them pull apart were the wolf calls from a group of teenage boys.

Beckett rested his forehead against hers. "I guess we're causing a spectacle."

"Yeah." She wrinkled her nose. "We seem to be making a habit of kissing in front of an audience."

He laughed, taking her hand. "Are you up for a few more times around the rink, then we'll get something to eat?"

"Yep, as long as you don't let go of my hand."

He winked. "No danger of that happening, Ava ..." He cocked his head, grinning. "You know? I don't even know your full name."

"Lawrence."

"Ava Lawrence," he mused. "I like it."

"Good," she giggled, feeling as buoyant as a balloon. "All right. Let's do this," she said with gusto.

He gave her a quizzical look, the corners of his lips turning down.

"What?" Her heart lurched. What had she done wrong?

"You didn't ask my last name."

Heat seeped into her face when she caught the tinge of hurt in his voice. "Oh, yeah. What is it?" *Crap!* She wasn't supposed to know his last name. She should've thought to ask.

"My last name's Bradshaw."

She forced a smile to cover the tension. "It's a good, solid sounding name. You have the alliteration thing going ... Beckett Bradshaw." Her voice sounded overly cheerful in her ears, a dead giveaway that she was overcompensating. Soon, Beckett would realize that she knew everything about him.

Thankfully, he relaxed. "Yeah, if you think my first and last name has the alliteration thing going, wait till you hear my middle name."

"Oh, yeah?"

"Beckett Bud Bradshaw," he said straight-faced.

She burst out laughing. "No, your mother wouldn't do that to you. Harmony seems like too reasonable of a woman for that."

A smile played on his lips. "Nah, she didn't. My real middle name's Christopher."

"Beckett Christopher Bradshaw." She knew that was correct, having seen it a few times. "I like it," she said emphatically.

He motioned with his head. "Shall we?"

"As long as you keep holding on to me."

He gave her a meaningful look. "Don't worry. I'll never let you go."

Warmth glowed through her as she flashed a giant smile. Oh, how she loved the sound of that. "Just so you know, I'm falling for you too, Beckett Christopher Bradshaw."

The next morning, Ava awoke to a blissful haze. Her date with Beckett the night before had been perfect. After ice skating, Beckett

walked her to her car where they drove to get his truck. Ava then
followed him to an Indian restaurant. They talked for a couple hours
about their growing-up years. Ava told about her life in Biloxi, Mississippi, leaving out the bad parts of her childhood. She shared about
her mother, how they used to bake together, and how her mother
loved to sing and dance. Beckett spoke of what it was like to grow up
in Park City with his brothers. "I'm the mixed-up middle child," he'd
said with a laugh. His eyes glowed with pride as he spoke of Jazzie,
how she was an honor student and played the clarinet in band.

The conversation had flowed easily. Before long, it was time to go.
Beckett walked her out to her BMW. To their delight, the dark
parking lot was empty except for the two of them. Beckett took full
advantage of the situation giving her a long, hard kiss that sent her
soaring to the stars. In fact, she was still dancing on air this morning.
Just thinking about that kiss sent tingles through to her toes.

Ava threw back the covers and got out of bed. Tonight, she was
going to Beckett's place where he was making her dinner. Sadly, the
following day, he'd begin to work a forty-eight-hour shift. She'd
teased him that she didn't know how she was going to entertain
herself in his absence. There was an element of truth to her words.
Now that Beckett was officially in her life, she didn't want to lose
him. Her stomach tightened. If her grandfather was alive, she'd insist
that they go back and redo everything. Beckett seemed content with
his life. The battle for that contentment had been hard fought. Ava
didn't want to turn everything upside down. The more she got to
know Beckett, the more she feared his reaction when everything took
place.

On her night stand was a framed picture of her grandparents. She
picked it up, touching her grandfather's face. "I fear we made a
mistake." A lump formed in her throat. "We wanted to do the right
thing, something good that would repay the good that was done to us,
but I don't know that we have."

She jumped when her phone rang. Hastily, she put down the
picture as she grabbed the phone. It was Houston calling. "Hello?"

Houston launched into the conversation without preamble. "I'm calling to let you know that I will be contacting Beckett Bradshaw in the next couple of days."

"No!" she exploded, clutching the phone. "You can't."

"I don't understand. That has been the plan all along. Is everything all right?"

"Yeah." She rubbed a hand across her forehead. Houston probably thought she was losing it. "It's just that ... well ... I hate to spring this on Beckett right now," she squeaked.

Houston let out a surprised chuckle. "There's no keeping a lid on this, Ava. Ted and Libby are chomping at the bit, demanding that I disclose the terms of the living trust. Time is of the essence here. The sooner I talk to Beckett, the better."

She needed more time with Beckett, precious time with him before everything changed. "Can you wait until after Christmas?"

"No, I'm afraid that's not possible."

Her mind whirled. "Okay, then give me a few more days."

"Why?"

A nervous laugh escaped her throat. "Please, Houston. Just a few more days."

Concern sounded in the older man's voice. "Ava, what's going on?"

Another call beeped in. Ava pulled the phone away from her ear and saw it was Beckett. "Uh, Houston. I've gotta let you go."

"This is important," he countered.

"We'll talk soon," she clipped, as she ended his call and switched over to Beckett. "Hello?" Her greeting sounded breathy and rushed.

"Good morning," Beckett said warmly, the timbre of his deep voice easing her nerves.

A large smile spread over her face. "Good morning."

"I miss you already."

"I miss you too."

"Too bad you have to work today."

She was so tempted to try and rearrange her client meetings, but knew that wouldn't go over well this close to Christmas. People were counting on her to get their homes ready for the holidays. She sighed. "I know. I'm sorry."

"No worries. It'll just make me appreciate you even more tonight. You sure I can't pick you up at your house?"

"Yes." The word came out more vehemently than she'd intended. She cringed at the silence that came over the line. "Beckett?"

"I'm here," he said flatly.

She wet her lips, her explanation tumbling out haphazardly. "It's just easier for me to come to your house. I have a late client meeting, and—"

"Ava? Why don't you want me to know where you live?"

Her heart shrived to the size of a pea. "I'm sorry." Her heart slammed out an erratic beat against her ribcage.

"What is it?"

"I just need time," she croaked, feeling as though the walls were closing in on her. First, Houston and now Beckett. It was too much to deal with this early in the morning.

"Time for what?" he pressed.

Her mouth grew drier than a fistful of cotton balls as she swallowed, clutching her throat. "I promise, if you'll just be patient—"

"Are you married?"

The question ripped her breath away as she gurgled. "What?" She pushed out a hard laugh. "No, of course not." It irritated her that Beckett would think so little of her.

Beckett let out a long breath. "I'm sorry, I don't mean to offend you." Long pause. "Everything's just going so great between us, that I don't want anything to mess it up."

"Amen," she piped in. Silence stretched between them. "Beckett, I care about you."

"I care about you too, Ava."

The tenderness in his words sent a glow of relief through her. Surely, it would be okay in the end. Beckett would see that she and her grandfather only had his best interest in mind. "I promise, soon, you'll understand why I'm hedging."

"Huh?"

She shook her head. "I wish I could explain it, but I can't right now." Her voice shook with intensity, eyes going moist. "All I can say is that I'm crazy about you." She balled her fist. *I've adored you for longer than you can imagine, and now, I'm falling hard!*

He chuckled. "That's good." He paused. "Does it scare you that things are happening so fast?"

She leaned back against the headboard, drawing her knees to her chest. "A little," she admitted. "Does it scare you?"

"Yes," he admitted quietly. "But, I wouldn't have it any other way."

"Neither would I."

"All right," he relented. "I'll give you time."

"Thank you," she breathed.

"See you tonight, beautiful."

"Yes, see you tonight."

CHAPTER 7

Beckett was no chef by any stretch of the imagination. When he first joined the PCFD, he couldn't boil water. However, after being forced to take his turn cooking meals, he'd learned how to make a couple decent recipes that he used over and over—tacos being at the top of the list. The zesty sauce of the bubbling taco meat tingled his nose as he stirred it. He wiped his hands on a dishtowel and began chopping lettuce, tomatoes, and onions.

His mind went back to the phone conversation he'd had this morning with Ava. He'd pressed her as much as he could about her reticence to share her address. At this point, he was left with only two choices—cut bait and move on, or be patient and let their relationship progress. He exhaled a long breath, knowing for him there was only one choice, the obvious one—see it through. He was invested, his feelings for Ava growing stronger every day. She felt the same way about him. A woman like Ava didn't come along every day. Heck, once in a lifetime. He wielded the knife through the lettuce with hard chops. Ava was amazing. He smiled, thinking of their ice skating experience. He'd felt like a champion, his hands on her waist as he supported her around the rink. He raked the lettuce into a bowl and reached for a tomato.

His phone buzzed. He reached for it, answering. "Hey, Jazzie."

His heart lurched at the muffled sob. "What's going on?"

Silence.

His body tensed as he put down the knife and braced his hand on the counter. "Jazzie?" he said louder. "What's going on?"

"Dave grounded me." Her voice caught as she hiccuped. "He's forcing me to spend the rest of the night in my room .... without dinner."

Anger flared through Beckett like a blow torch. "What?"

The only sound on the line was a string of muffled sobs.

Beckett pushed a hand through his hair. "What happened?"

"I was out shopping with Macy. Her mom was late picking us up." Her voice broke as she drew in a hoarse breath. "I got home late and missed the first part of dinner." Her voice rose. "Dave ordered me to my room and told me I could forget about dinner."

Beckett wanted to punch a hole through the wall. No other man had the right to keep his daughter from eating dinner. It took all the effort he could summon to keep his voice even. "What did your mother say about it?"

"She agreed with Dave." Jazzie's voice sounded small and wounded.

Beckett's skin crawled as he clenched his teeth, shaking his head. He glanced at the clock. Ava was due to arrive any minute. "All right, honey. Hang tight. I'll call your mother and find out what's going on."

"Can you come and get me?"

"Let me talk to your mother first."

Jazzie sniffled. "All right."

"I'll call you back soon, sweetheart."

"Thanks, Dad," she squeaked as he ended the call.

He called Melinda and cursed under his breath when it went to voicemail. Rather than leaving a message, he called her again. Same thing, voicemail. He called a third and fourth time. She answered on the fifth.

"Hello?" she huffed.

"Why did Dave send Jazzie to her room with no dinner?" he demanded.

A stunned silence came over the line. "Did Jazzie call you?" Melinda sounded outraged.

He charged in, his words beating out an accusing cadence. "Yes, she did. I've tried to be as patient as I can with Dave, but he has no right to keep Jazzie from eating dinner."

"Dave is doing the best he can to maintain order in our home."

"Not at the expense of my daughter," Beckett roared.

The doorbell rang. *Great! Perfect timing.* Earlier today, Beckett sent Ava a text telling her he'd leave the door unlocked downstairs, so she could come on up to his loft.

Melinda's voice escalated. "What did Jazzie tell you?"

"Hang on."

"No, I will not hang on," Melinda responded indignantly. "You have no right to call up, accusing Dave of things when you don't have all the facts."

"There's someone at the door. Hang on!" he said, talking over her.

This is not how Beckett pictured this evening going. He went to the door with the phone cradled on his shoulder. He opened it, forcing a smile. "Hey."

"Hey," Ava said breezily, a large smile on her face. The smile faded when she saw his expression. "Is everything okay?"

He waved her in. "Sorry, I'm in the middle of a call. Have a seat."

Ava nodded, removing her coat as went over to the sofa and sat down.

"Oh, so you've got company." Melinda chortled out a bitter laugh. "Jazzie said you had a new woman in your life. Well, I hope for your sake and hers that you don't have any undue pressures in your life. Otherwise, the fairy tale will go up in a puff of putrid smoke."

The comment hit him like a punch in the gut, nearly stealing his breath away. For a second, he was at a loss for words. He glanced at Ava who was sitting sideways on the couch, her hand resting on the back as she watched him, a look of deep concern on her face. "How could you say something like that?" Beckett asked. "You know how hard I've worked to get where I am." His words lost air as he swallowed. "I've done my best to respect you and Dave." His voice shook with restrained fury. "I would hope that you would do the same for me."

Melinda let out a long breath. "You're right. I'm sorry. I just get so sick of Jazzie playing us against each other."

His brows drew together. "What do you mean?"

"Did Jazzie tell you why Dave sent her to her room without dinner?"

"Yes, she and Macy went shopping and Macy's mom was late picking them up. I don't think that is cause to punish Jazzie." His voice rose. He glanced at Ava, could tell this conversation was making her uncomfortable. Well, that's just how it was. Jazzie would always have to come first.

Melinda punched out the words like she was driving home a point. "Yes, Kathy was late picking up Jazzie and Macy because they weren't at the designated meeting spot when she arrived."

"Huh?"

"Neither Jazzie nor Macy answered her repeated calls. Kathy drove around the perimeter of the mall, looking for them. She was about to call the police when she spotted them outside an arcade talking to a couple of boys."

Beckett's chest squeezed. "What?"

"Oh, it gets worse," Melinda retorted. "The boys were older and vaping."

Beckett choked out a strangled cough. "What?"

"Now, you know why Dave sent Jazzie to bed without dinner." Her voice grew brittle. "He was probably trying to avert disaster, keep me from killing the little punk."

"Why didn't you call me?"

"I was planning to, tomorrow."

"Wow." Beckett still found it hard to believe that Jazzie would do such a thing and then twist it around to make Melinda and Dave look like the bad guys. "What should we do about this?"

She blew out a heavy breath. "I'm not sure. Luckily, all Jazzie and

Macy were doing was talking. They claim to have just met the guys. Beckett, we can't let this continue—Jazzie using us against each other."

He rubbed a hand across his forehead. "Yeah, you're right. I'm sorry I overreacted. I should've gotten all of the facts first."

Long pause. "I'm sorry for what I said. That was low. If you've found someone ... well, that's a good thing."

He heard the regret in Melinda's voice, knew she wished things could've turned out different between them.

"I'm happy for you, Beckett, truly," Melinda said.

"Thanks." Beckett was happy for himself too. Notwithstanding whatever Ava was holding back, she was the find of a lifetime. He looked at Ava, so stunningly beautiful in a royal blue sweater, her blonde hair gleaming like gold. Her features were pulled with concern over him. No, not just him. She pointed behind him. At the same instant, he smelled something burning. "Crapola! The taco meat!" He looked at the stove, not knowing whether to laugh or cry. Black smoke billowed from the skillet. He turned off the stovetop and removed the skillet, waving a hand to clear the smoke.

"What's wrong?" Melinda asked.

"Nothing," he said sarcastically. "Except for the fact that my dinner is now burnt to a crisp." He gave Ava an apologetic look.

Ava shook her head, her eyes going wider than quarters.

Melinda laughed darkly. "I'm sorry." She didn't sound sorry though. She sounded kind of glad. Melinda was fine with her having a new husband if Beckett remained single and alone. She was selfish that way. A small woman in many ways. Still, she was the mother of his daughter. In this instance, she was right. Beckett would've sent Jazzie to bed without dinner too. There was no excuse for Jazzie's actions. "I've gotta let you go," he said to Melinda. "We'll talk about this tomorrow." He ended the call at the same instant the smoke detector went off. He coughed to clear his lungs as he reached for a cookie sheet to fan the smoke. Ava jumped up, coming into the kitchen. "What can I do to help?"

The loud squeal of the smoke detector pierced Beckett's ears. He winced, ducking slightly. "Quick! Open the front door." He strode into the attached living room and opened a window to create a cross wind. A second later, he grabbed a chair and disconnected the alarm.

Several minutes later, most of the smoke had cleared. He reached for the skillet of charred meat and placed it in the sink, running cold water over it.

Ava stepped beside him and placed a hand on his arm. "Are you okay?"

"Yeah." He laughed an apology. "Well, there went our dinner."

"It smelled amazing." The corners of her lips quivered like she was trying not to laugh. "Before it became a charred brick." She motioned with her eyes at the skillet.

He leaned back against the counter, a lopsided grin tugging at his lips. "So, much for impressing you, huh?"

"Oh, I'm already sufficiently impressed."

Her comment surprised him, pleased him. "Really?"

"Really." Her blue eyes shimmered with laughter. "I mean, it's not every day I get to watch a fireman set his own kitchen ablaze."

He chuckled dryly. "Yeah, that's one for the books." He rubbed his jaw. "My fire crew would have a heyday with this."

Ava made a zipping motion across her lips. "Your secret's safe with me."

He turned to face her, gathering her in his arms. "Did I tell you how incredible you look tonight?"

She flashed a pleased smile, her dimples showing. "No, you didn't."

"Well, you do. When I saw you, my world stopped turning."

"That's putting it on a little thick."

"It's true. Everything changed the moment I saw you at the bowling alley."

Something indiscernible flashed in her eyes. Ava was intriguing, perplexing, the kind of woman Beckett could spend a lifetime getting to know.

"For me too," she said seriously.

"Is that a good thing?"

Her smile was automatic. "Yes." She gave him a tender look. "I feel so blessed that you're in my life."

"I feel the same," he said emphatically. "At the risk of scaring you away, do I dare admit that I can't stop thinking about you? You're magnificent."

"Thanks," she murmured, her lashes brushing against her high cheekbones. The movement was subtle, yet so feminine. "I might've been thinking about you too," she said shyly.

He laughed, contentment wrapping euphoric threads around him. "That's a good thing. I'd hate to think this was a one-way street."

She squared her chin. "Definitely not."

Somehow Beckett knew in that moment that Ava was in his life to stay. For her, he really could be the stand-up man she deserved. He could stay the course, keep his demons at bay. He wanted that, more than he wanted air.

Ava looked up at Beckett, placing a hand on his jaw. "What's going on with Jazzie?"

The tenderness in her voice struck a chord in Beckett. He was so grateful Ava had come into his life. If he could've found the Fruitcake Lady, he would've given her a kiss on the cheek, proclaiming that her prophecy was right. He had found love by Christmas—before Christmas, actually.

"What're you thinking about? You have an amused look on your face."

Someday, he'd tell Ava about the Fruitcake Lady, but not tonight. Better wait on that one. He didn't want Ava to think he was a nut job. He laughed easily. "Oh, nothing important. Just how crazy this night has been." He drew in a breath. "Back to Jazzie," he said, telling Ava everything.

"I'm sorry," she began, "it must be hard to be in your situation, having to depend on your ex-wife and her husband to make the right decisions for Jazzie."

"Yes, it is. Jazzie's always been such a good girl. She's been through so much." Guilt stabbed at him as Melinda's harsh words came rushing back. Could he do this? Could he hold it together in a new relationship? Life was bound to have pressures. Sometimes he felt like a ticking bomb, set to go off when everything was going well in his life. He pushed aside the fears. He could do this. With Ava by his side, he could do anything.

"Jazzie's a good girl," Ava said firmly. "She's just testing the water."

"Yes, that she is. Speaking of which, I guess I need to call her back." He gave Ava a pained look. "I'm sorry. This evening isn't turning out how I'd hoped."

"Don't worry, I'm fine. We're here together. That's what counts, right?"

"Right." His shoulders released some of their tension, his eyes moving over her beautiful face. "I'm glad you're here with me."

"Me too."

"I guess we'll have to order pizza," he said dejectedly.

She laughed. "There are worse things we could eat. Pizza's one of my favorites," she assured him. "Why don't I order it while you call Jazzie back?"

He reached in his pocket and pulled out his wallet. "Let me give you my credit card."

"I don't mind getting it," Ava said casually.

"No, you will absolutely not," he countered. "What kind of man would I be if I invited you to my house for dinner and made you pay for it?"

She rolled her eyes. "All right." She took his card, stepping away from him. "By the way, your place looks great. I love the open space and large windows." She pointed at the stacked canvases against the wall. "Are those yours?"

"Yes." It felt so personal, to have his work inspected. Normally, he preferred to keep his art to himself. However, he realized that he wanted Ava to see them, wanted her to know who he was.

"I'll have to check them out."

"I've been meaning to hang them, but haven't gotten around to it." There were so many other unfinished projects commanding his attention. Beckett had purchased a commercial building off the main street of Park City and converted the upper section into a loft apartment. He'd toyed with renting out the bottom section to a business, but right now, it was empty. "It's definitely a work in progress." He gave her a teasing look. "I'm sure it could use the services of an interior designer."

An amused smile curled her lips. "I'll see if I can find one for you."

She had a wonderful voice, soft and silky with just the right amount of moxie. "Uh, huh," he drawled. He let her get a couple of steps away before tugging on her hand. She raised an eyebrow, glancing back over her shoulder. "Come here," he implored, turning her around to face him. "The pizza and art can wait," he uttered, reaching for the card and placing it on the counter. He slid his arms around her waist, drawing her close. Tenderly, he pushed back a lock of her hair, cupping her cheek. His gaze traced the outline of her full, sultry lips. With deliberate slowness, he brushed his lips against her forehead. Her breath caught as she closed her eyes. Lightly, he kissed her nose before his mouth covered hers. Passion burned a hot flame through him as he ran his hands over her back and up through her glorious hair. She tilted her head back, fully accepting the demands of his lips. Beckett had the sensation of rocketing into space in a blaze of brilliance as their lips moved together. With that brilliance came a feeling of completeness, like coming home to a place he hadn't realized existed.

When the kiss was over, he pulled back, savoring the details of her delicately carved face. She was a curious mixture of softness and inherent strength. "You are something," he said softly, twisting a finger around a tendril of her hair.

A light laugh floated like a summer breeze from her throat. "Back at ya, Superman."

Pleasure hummed through his veins. "Superman, huh?"

She wiggled her eyebrows, assessing him. "Yep. I've never met a man who was more fitting of the description."

He thought she might've been teasing, but was touched when he saw the sincerity in her sapphire eyes. "Thank you," he said in surprise.

She gave him a reassuring smile. "I know it's tough with Jazzie, but you'll figure it out." Her smile widened. "I have a feeling you can handle anything that's thrown your way."

If only that were the case. His stomach tightened, knowing that he'd have to come clean about his past. What would Ava think when she learned the truth about him? Would she still look at him with adoring eyes, like he was the greatest thing on the planet? Or, would she regard him with a hostile pity like Melinda had done?

Concern touched Ava's features. "What's wrong?"

He needed to tell her the truth, but he didn't want to. Could he just keep the past to himself? Even as the thought raced through his head, his mouth started moving. "There's something I need to tell you."

"Okay," she said carefully.

His phone buzzed. He chuckled humorlessly. "Perfect timing, huh?" He pulled away from her to reach for it. "It's Jazzie," he explained.

She nodded in understanding. "Go ahead. I'll order the pizza while you talk to her."

His jaw tightened, knowing it wouldn't be a pleasant conversation, but it had to take place.

CHAPTER 8

Having ordered the pizza, Ava made her way over to the stack of canvases against the wall. An unexpected gush of emotion swept over Ava as she looked through them. Most were of people living on the streets. Each painting offered a unique angle of the plight of human suffering. One held her attention—an older woman, her face bunched in leathery wrinkles. A tattered blanket was draped around her shriveled frame, her claw-like fingers clutching the sides as she tried to draw into herself. The vacant look in her watery, silver eyes had a haunting, empty quality. The woman's meager belongings were littered around her, along with a thin, forlorn dog on a leash, huddled beside her.

Tears misted Ava's eyes as she blinked. It was one thing to hear about Beckett's time on the streets but quite another to see these paintings. The suffering was so up-close and personal. No one, except for a person who'd lived it, could capture the suffering so completely. Yes, he was a skilled artist, as his mother had said. However, the art was secondary to the subjects. Ava wondered if the art was a form of therapy for Beckett. Maybe it was easier to paint it than talk about it.

She glanced back at Beckett who was still on the phone with Jazzie. The conversation had been heated, at first. Now, Beckett was speaking in a calmer tone. If things with Beckett went as Ava hoped, she would have a relationship with Jazzie and would have to learn to navigate the constant emotional swings of a pre-teen. *One step at a time.* There was no sense in worrying about that right now. She and Beckett had plenty of troubled water to get through first.

A little while later after the pizza was eaten, Ava and Beckett relaxed on the couch. Ava snuggled into the curve of Beckett's shoulder, appreciating the protective feel of his arm around her. A Christmas movie was playing on the TV, but she'd hardly paid attention to it because her mind was so consumed with Beckett.

He stroked her hair, glancing at the unfinished fireplace insert. "I'm sorry the fireplace isn't working."

A smile played on her lips. "Remember who you're talking to. I'm used to works in progress."

"I imagine you are," he chuckled, angling to face her. "How did you first get into design work?"

Ava pursed her lips as she gathered her thoughts. She wanted to tell Beckett all about her life. She wanted him to know everything about her, as she did him. If she told him part of the story tonight, it would make it easier when Beckett learned the rest. "Before I went to live with my dad and grandparents, I was raised by my mother Willow."

"Willow," Beckett mused. "That's an interesting name."

"Yes, it was very fitting. My mother was an unusual person."

Interest lit his dark eyes. "How so?"

"She and my dad had a fling in college at UCLA. Until I was a teenager, I didn't even know who my dad was. He didn't know I even existed until my mom called him asking for money." The sympathetic look on Beckett's face was moving.

"I'm sorry."

She shrugged. "It's okay. It was just my life, ya know?"

He nodded.

"You asked me why I went into interior design. Well, I suppose part of the reason was to fix something inside myself."

He cocked his head. "What do you mean?"

She moistened her dry lips. "Well, my mom and I were poor. We lived in a rundown house. I was embarrassed about it." She sighed heavily. "As crazy as it sounds, now, every time I help someone fix up their home, I'm righting something inside of me." She laughed tonelessly. "I know it sounds crazy."

"No, not at all. I totally understand where you're coming from."

She could see in Beckett's eyes that he got her, in a way few others could. She suspected that he was the same. Helping people helped fix the broken part of him. She braced herself, not knowing how Beckett would react to the rest. It was better for him to hear it from her. "My mother was fun, spontaneous, brilliant."

Beckett gave her a smile filled with such tenderness that it caused her heart to melt. "The apple doesn't fall far from the tree," he beamed.

"In some ways." She forced her mouth to push the words out. "My mother was an alcoholic."

The sudden intake of Beckett's breath was the only sound in the room. She felt him tense as his features went rigid.

Her words tumbled out. "Shortly after my dad found out about me, my mom was killed in a car accident. She was drunk and weaved into the oncoming traffic, hitting a car head-on. The father of the family was killed instantly." Having lived with the horror of the event most of her life, she spoke the words dispassionately, as if cold reading the lines of play. "They were headed to have dinner with relatives. I went to live with my dad." Her voice quivered. "I spent two wonderful years with my dad until he died suddenly from his degenerative heart defect. After that, I was raised by my grandparents." She exhaled in relief at having gotten it out.

Beckett's face was ashen, his jaw clenched. The agonized expression on his rugged face cut her to the core. She could only imagine what must be running through his mind right now. She gave him a searching look. "Are you okay?" She had to keep reminding herself that she wasn't supposed to know about his past. He removed his arm as he scooted forward on the couch, clenching his hands. She touched his arm. "Beckett?"

"I can't imagine how hard it must be to have lost your grandfather recently."

She swallowed. "Yes."

He let out a long breath, his jaw working. "Remember when I said earlier that there was something I needed to tell you? And then the phone rang?"

"Yes." She wanted him to get it off his chest, so she could let him know it was okay. He rubbed his jaw, a look of self-loathing overtaking his features. The transformation was unsettling. "Whatever it is, it will be okay," she said soothingly.

"No," he growled. "It won't."

She had to fight the temptation to speak, knew instinctively that she had to allow him space to get it out.

He looked at the ceiling, letting out a short grunt, before looking at her. "I'm also an alcoholic."

Fear seized her. "What?" She'd thought that was in the past, that he was a changed man. Had she and her grandfather been wrong?

He pushed out a humorless laugh. "I don't drink anymore, but I'll always have the weakness. A recovering alcoholic."

A heady relief swept over her. "I'm glad you were able to overcome it."

He nodded absently, going straight back to the narrative, his eyes taking on a faraway look. "I wasn't always a fireman." His eyes locked with hers, pleading for understanding. "Before ... I worked at a financial company in downtown Salt Lake, as a hedge fund manager." He shook his head in disgust. "I was naïve, ambitious, determined to make my mark on the world. I was over-confident, took unnecessary risks, lost a great deal of my clients' money. The stress got to me, and I started drinking."

She felt his pain as if it were her own, circling around her, squeezing like an anaconda.

"One afternoon, I picked up Jazzie from dance." He coughed to clear the emotion. "I was drunk, ran a red light and got t-boned. I walked away without a scratch." His voice hitched. "Jazzie wasn't so lucky. Her ankle was crushed, so severely that the doctors feared she'd never walk again."

"You'd never know by looking at her now."

He smiled grimly. "I know. It's a miracle." He clasped and unclasped his hands. "I thank God every day that she's all right." Tears rose in his eyes as he swallowed. "After the accident, I went off the deep end, lived on the streets for a few months." He shrugged. "Eventually, I got my life straightened out. And well ..." he gave her a pained smile "... here we are."

"Yes, here we are."

His lips formed a tight line. "I'll understand if you don't want anything else to do with me," he said morosely.

She chuckled. "You don't think you're getting rid of me that easily, do you?"

He jerked in surprise. "But, how could you want to be with me after what I told you?" His eyes hardened. "Like your mom, I could've been that drunk that cost another person's life."

"But you didn't. The people in the other car were all okay," she argued. "Jazzie's doing great too."

"Yes, I was lucky."

"And blessed," she added.

"That too." He stopped, tipping his head. "How did you know the people in the other car were okay? I never told you that."

Heat fanned her face. "You didn't?"

"No." His brows drew together as he gave her a suspicious look.

"I guess I just assumed." She knew how lame her explanation sounded. Briefly, she wondered if she should just tell him everything tonight, here and now, while they were opening up to one another. No, she couldn't do that. She'd promised her grandfather that she'd let it come from Houston. Her grandfather wanted everything to be done in proper order so there'd be no snags. She flashed an apologetic smile. "Sorry, I shouldn't have just assumed ..." Her voice trailed off.

He gave her an incredulous look. "I can't believe you still want me, now that you know the truth."

"Yeah, it's hard to hear what you've been through, but of course, I want you." She touched his cheek. "I told you over the phone, I'm falling for you, Superman. Hard and fast. There's no getting away from me now."

"That's good," he said, the deep, velvety tone of his voice reverberating contentment through her as he took her in his arms for another hungry kiss that seared a path straight to her heart.

I love you, she said in her mind as she lost herself in the feel of his lips.

Normally, Beckett enjoyed spending time with his fire crew family and their usual lighthearted banter, but it had been a long couple of days without Ava. It was a little after six a.m., and the guys from the other shift would start trickling in around 6:30 for the official passing of the torch at seven. Taking the last bite of his cereal, he drained the remaining milk and went to wash the bowl and spoon. Beckett was looking forward to having a few days off so he could spend some time with Ava.

Work had been grueling. They'd responded to four car accidents and a couple of medical emergencies. Last night was the worst because there was a traffic fatality. After the call, Beckett gathered the facts. A young mother was headed to an all-night pharmacy to pick up medicine for her sick child when she collided with another car. Her husband was home with all the children, awaiting her return. Beckett hated thinking of the hardship the father and kids would face, especially so soon before Christmas. That was the tough part of this job—separating his personal feelings. Of course, the fact that he didn't get back to the station and to sleep until three a.m. didn't help matters. He was up again at 5:45. doing his part to get the station ready for the next shift. It was interesting, being a firefighter had its own element of stress, but it was different from the stress he'd been under as a hedge fund manager. Here, he felt valued and needed, accepted by the crew; whereas, in his other job everything was a battle. Nothing he did was ever good enough to please his boss. Also, he'd never been able to satisfy Melinda's desire for more material wealth and status. It had been a hollow, frustrating existence. He hugged his arms, grateful that part of his life was now behind him.

Even his lack of sleep couldn't douse his optimism about his wonderful future with Ava. He still couldn't believe Ava had been so understanding about his past. When she first told him about her mother, his insides had collapsed fearing their budding relationship would erupt into a ball of flames. She didn't even seem that surprised about his past. She took everything in stride, rolling with the punches. Ava was the kind of woman Beckett wanted by his side, a partner in every way.

His thoughts moved to Jazzie. The night she was quarantined to her room, he'd given her a severe tongue-lashing over the phone, telling her that he agreed with Dave and Melinda. Jazzie going to bed without dinner was a small price to pay for her actions. The next day, Melinda grounded her. Jazzie was still peeved about that, but she'd come around. Beckett was learning that he needed to take a firmer hand with Jazzie. No way could she continue pitting him and Melinda against each other. Being a parent of a pre-teen wasn't for the faint hearted. Beckett was sure he'd have many more battles to fight on that front before it was over.

He sighed. That's the way life was. You get one part of it figured out and another gives you trouble. At least he had Ava in his life.

"Look at you over there grinning like a possum," Charlotte said.

Was he grinning? Beckett hadn't even realized. He glanced at the kitchen table where his crew members were sitting, enjoying a quick breakfast together before the shift change.

"It's probably just a glazed-over look from lack of sleep," Nikola added, rising to wash his bowl and spoon.

Jak tipped his head, studying him critically as if he were a painting in a museum. "Nah, has to be a woman."

Beckett felt the burn of heat over his face, knew he was shining like a sunburn. He went back to the table and plopped down.

A shrewd smile spread over Garrett's lips. "Beckett's got himself a woman," he taunted.

"I guess the Fruitcake Lady wasn't too far off with her love prophecy, huh?" Charlotte teased, shoving Beckett's arm.

Beckett chuckled. "I plead the fifth." He'd not breathed a word about Ava to the crew. Mostly because he knew they'd tease him relentlessly. Also, he wanted to hold the newness of the relationship close to himself for a while longer.

Jak shifted in his seat. "Who is this mystery lady?"

"I never said there was a lady," Beckett countered stubbornly.

"You didn't have to," Charlotte hooted. "It's written all over your face."

The doorbell chimed. They all looked at each other.

"Who the heck could that be this time of the morning?" Garrett grumbled.

Beckett made a face. "It couldn't be the other shift. They have IDs."

Nikola rolled his eyes. "Unless one of them forgot their card. You know how lax A Platoon is." He looked at Garrett. "Cap would roast us if we forgot our card."

"Dang straight," Garrett quipped, his jaw set in a firm stance.

Beckett grinned inwardly. Just as it should be, all of them thought that PCFD 3 C, their crew, was the best. They did everything right. The other crews were slackers.

A cheeky grin spread over Charlotte's lips. "Maybe it's Beckett's mystery woman."

Beckett rolled his eyes, secretly glad they were joking around. They were all sleep deprived. Not to mention that the car accident earlier had jarred the entire crew, especially him and Charlotte who, as the medics, had been hands-on with the patient while the rest of the crew worked on extrication.

"Come on, Beckett," Garrett urged. "Spill it. We know you have a girl."

"How about you, old man? You've been awfully interested in going to Piper's school lately." Piper was Garrett's daughter. Beckett suspected that Garrett had a thing for her first-grade teacher. The deep red blush of Garrett's face let Beckett know he'd hit the nail on the head.

"Ooh, do tell," Charlotte chimed, eyes shimmering interest.

Beckett was relieved the attention shifted away from him. Garrett shot him an irritated look. "Thanks a lot, man."

"Anytime," he said pleasantly.

The doorbell rang again.

Beckett rose from his chair. "I'll get it," he said in a singsong voice.

"Good because it's probably your woman," Charlotte said, pumping her eyebrows as her voice went juicy. "She's been pining away for you," she said dramatically, placing a hand over her chest. "She couldn't wait forty minutes until you got off, she had to come rushing here to see you."

"Yeah, yeah," Beckett said dryly. He went to the door and opened it, surprised to see a tall man about his same height standing before him. The man looked to be in his early seventies with a shock of snow white hair, bushy brows, and a handlebar mustache. Never having seen him before, Beckett was surprised when the man's face lit with recognition.

"Beckett Bradshaw," he said in a deep, booming voice, "just the man I wanted to see."

The man had a drawl, like he was from Texas. Beckett frowned. "I'm sorry? Do I know you?" Beckett shivered at the cold blast of wind.

"Nope, we've never met. I'm Houston Thomas. Is there somewhere we can talk?"

"Now? We're just about to change shifts. Things are kind of hectic right now."

Houston's feet remained firmly planted, his expression unyielding. "It's important."

Beckett let out a breath. "All right. Come in."

Houston stepped inside and closed the door behind him.

"What's up?" Garrett asked, stepping up and looking Houston up and down, a deep furrow carved between his brows.

"I'm not sure," Beckett answered, looking back at Houston.

"It's personal business," Houston said tersely, tugging at his coat. Clearly, he wasn't used to having to explain himself. "I just need a minute of your time."

Garrett raised an eyebrow, pointing to his chest. "My time?" His gaze lingered on Houston's pointy-toed, snake-skin boots underneath his white pants.

"No, his," Houston said, pointing at Beckett.

Beckett looked at Garrett and shrugged as if to say, *I have no idea what this is about.*

"We'll be in the community room," Beckett said as Garrett headed back up the stairs. When they stepped into the room, he motioned at the long table and chairs. "Have a seat."

Houston removed his coat and placed it on the back of one of the chairs. Beckett bit back a smile when he saw the white suit. Houston could've been a dead-ringer for the KFC restaurant icon Colonel Sanders. He was wearing a Western-style tie with black cords, the ends tipped in silver metal. The cords were held together by a round, silver clasp with a turquoise stone in the center. In a dignified manner, Houston sat down and crossed his legs, straightening the pleats on his pants. Beckett also sat down. He couldn't imagine what this could be about.

"I'm here on official business," Houston began, "representing my late client Milton McQueen."

Houston's voice was deep and melodic like the actor Morgan Freeman. *Milton McQueen.* Why did that name sound familiar?

"He owned McQueen Capital Group," Houston supplied.

"The real estate investment company?"

"Yes."

Ah. That's where he'd heard it, in his other life in the financial world. McQueen Capital Group was a powerhouse whose ambition was to acquire key commercial properties around the globe. He rubbed his jaw. "What does this have to do with me?"

They heard the murmur of someone talking and then Nikola

came in, pulling the phone away from his ear. "Hey, Beck, you seen my iPad?"

"No, man, I haven't."

Nikola frowned. "I know it's around here somewhere." He offered a casual wave to Houston. "Sorry to interrupt."

Houston just sat there, a stern expression on his face. Beckett smiled. "No worries. It's all good."

Nikola nodded, leaving as quickly as he'd come.

Houston tugged on his tie clasp as he leaned forward, speaking in a low tone. "It's better if we continue this conversation somewhere more private. My office." He reached in his pocket and pulled out a card, sliding it across the table to Beckett. "Here's the address. Meet me there later today."

Beckett picked up the card. This whole thing was odd. Very odd.

Houston scooted back his chair with a loud scrape, then stood, buttoning his suit jacket. "Shall we say one o'clock?"

Beckett rose to his feet. "Before we go any farther, I need to know what this is about." He squared his jaw, eyeing Houston.

A hint of amusement glittered in the older man's eyes. "All I can tell you at this point is that it would be in your best interest to be there," he said crisply, reaching for his coat and draping it over his arm. He offered a curt nod.

Beckett watched, befuddled, as Houston strode out. The elderly man's carriage spoke of grandeur, like he was a gentleman of a bygone time. "Strange duck," he muttered, turning the card over in his hand. Beckett was getting together with Jazzie at three to take her Christmas shopping. This evening, he planned to go to dinner with Ava. There was no reason why he couldn't meet Houston at his office; although he would've appreciated it if the man had asked him to come, rather than summoning him. If he didn't go, curiosity would prick away at him. Houston said he represented the late Milton McQueen, meaning the real estate tycoon had passed away. He exhaled a long sigh, wishing Houston had just come out with what-ever it was he had to say, saving Beckett the trouble of going to the man's office. Oh, well, after he got some sleep he was heading into

Salt Lake anyway to pick up Jazzie. He'd just leave a little earlier and stop by Houston's office first.

Whatever this was, it had better be good.

Hot prickles covered him. This wasn't some throwback from his time as a hedge fund manager, was it? He'd never done any work for McQueen Capital Group. It was possible that one of his clients had connections with McQueen. There were so many hidden ties between people and companies that it was hard to tell who was connected. Was this some sort of retribution for the money he'd lost? If so, why come after him now, after all this time? Could anyone come after him? Sure, he'd lost money because of bad judgement and taking unnecessary risks, but everything had been on the up-and-up. Clients entered agreements with the understanding that no investments were guaranteed.

He shoved the card into his pocket as he walked back up the stairs to grab his things and say bye to the crew. Before Houston's arrival, he'd been light as air, excited about getting off work to spend time with Ava and Jazzie. Now, he was apprehensive about what business Houston had to discuss with him. Anytime a man threw around terms like, *"It would be in your best interest to be there,"* Beckett grew concerned.

The more he thought about it, the more convinced he became that whatever this was about—wasn't good.

CHAPTER 9

In moments like these, the only thing Ava could do was apologize. "I'm so sorry, Mrs. Benson." She truly was sorry. Ava never would've recommended the painting crew had she known they were such derelicts.

"Clint and I use you because we trust you. The contractors you've recommended in the past have been wonderful, but this ..." she shook her head "... this is unacceptable." Her voice quivered with intensity. "Clint doesn't need this stress right now, with him recovering from his heart attack."

"I know. You're absolutely right," Ava said fiercely. "I just put in a call to Mason Winthrop, the owner of Winthrop Painting. Rest assured, I'll get to the bottom of this."

Fire shot from Mrs. Benson's eyes. "Under no condition are Mitch and Randy to ever step foot in my house again."

Ava's jaw tightened. "Don't worry, there's no chance of that happening."

"If the paint won't come out of my rug, I'm going to expect it to be replaced."

"Absolutely." Ava was mortified when she received a frantic call from Mrs. Benson. The two painters were supposed to show up at eight a.m. to work on her home. Instead, they showed up at ten, both sloppily drunk. As they were painting the walls in Mrs. Benson's living room, they got into a fistfight, with one of them accusing the other of stealing his Mtn Dews from the cooler. During their scuffle, they knocked over a can of paint that spilled on Mrs. Benson's ten-thousand-dollar Oriental Rug. Thankfully, the paint was latex. Had it been oil, they wouldn't have had a prayer of getting it out. The other bright spot was that Winthrop Painting was bonded and insured. Otherwise, Ava or Mason Winthrop would have to cough up money to cover the rug. Ava took great pains to recommend good contractors. She'd been working with Mason Winthrop for years. He was a good man, but had fallen short on this one. At the end of the day, the buck stopped with the owner and his poor choice of employees.

The goal at this point was to salvage her relationship with Mrs. Benson. Her phone rang. "That's probably Winthrop now." Nope, it was Houston, probably trying to talk her into giving the okay for him to contact Beckett. That wasn't going to happen. She was going to insist that Houston wait until after Christmas to speak to Beckett. She let the call go to voicemail. "Sorry, it's not Winthrop. I'll keep trying until I get him though. The rug cleaner should be here soon." Knowing time was of the essence, Ava had used a towel to soak up the excess paint and then came behind it with a wet cloth. She didn't want to rub too hard for fear of breaking down the wool fibers of the rug. Better to let the cleaners do their thing.

"What about my living room?" Mrs. Benson grumbled. "It was supposed to be done today. I've got company coming into town, tomorrow, for Christmas."

"I promise, I'll do everything in my power to get someone else out here to finish the job." Why wasn't Winthrop calling her back? She'd left him two voice messages and three texts. Obviously, it was time to start looking for another painting company. Ava would be hard pressed to find anyone to come in at the last minute, so close to Christmas. Her best hope was to play on Winthrop's sense of ethics and his desire to keep her happy. She'd sent him a lot of work over the years.

Her phone rang again. "It's Winthrop," she said to Mrs. Benson. "Hey," she began, "we've got a big problem."

An hour later, Ava managed to sort through the mess. Winthrop spoke to Mrs. Benson personally, assuring her that he'd have another painter there within a few hours to finish the job. The rug cleaner guy felt sure he could get the remainder of the paint out without damaging the rug. He'd bundled it up, taking it with him to his shop. Supposedly, he'd have it back by tomorrow. Ava hoped that was the case.

Her mind ticked through her to-do list. She had enough time to grab a quick lunch at her favorite sushi restaurant. Afterwards, she'd head to a furniture store off Highland Drive where she would help a client select the style and fabric for a custom sofa. That was it for her work today. After that, she planned to go shopping for a new outfit to wear tonight. The thought of seeing Beckett again was enough to erase the headache of her morning. She smiled, thinking of the text he'd sent her earlier, saying he couldn't wait to see her.

Her eyes widened as she tightened her hold on the steering wheel. Houston had called her at Mrs. Benson's house. She should probably listen to his voicemail. She pushed the touch screen on her dash, playing the message.

"Hey, it's me." He paused. "I wanted to let you know that I spoke to Beckett at his fire station this morning."

"What?!" she exclaimed. "No!" Fury spiked through her as she hit the center of the steering wheel.

"Beckett's meeting me at the office today at 1:00. There's no reason to keep putting this off. The longer it sits, the harder it'll be for everyone." Another pause. "All right. That's it." He ended the call.

Tears rose in Ava's eyes. This couldn't be happening! She glanced at the clock on her dash. 12:40. It would take at least thirty minutes to get downtown.

Her mind raced. Should she try calling Beckett? No, she couldn't tell him over the phone. She had to get there! Had to! All thoughts of her impending client meeting flew out of her head as she pushed the accelerator, weaving around the car in front of her.

Ten minutes later, she let out a cry of dismay when she heard the siren and saw the blue lights. Renegade thoughts of outrunning the officer whirled through her mind. No, that would be stupid. She let out a hard laugh. Just her luck!

Having no other choice, she pulled over.

Standing on the sidewalk, looking up at the imposing glass and metal building, Beckett felt like he was thrust back in time. McQueen Capital Group was located two blocks from where he used to work at W. Shields Financial Group. He glanced down, his attire of a jacket, jeans, and casual work boots putting him at ease. He was no longer that other man. He'd find out what the deal was with Houston Thomas and would be on his way.

He offered a silent prayer, asking for help to move his feet forward through the double-glass doors. A second later, he put on his game face and strode in where a woman was sitting behind a reception booth. "Hello. How may I help you?" Her disapproving eyes flickered over him, shouting loud and clear that he wasn't appropriately dressed. For some reason, the woman's snub helped ease his jitters a fraction.

It registered in his mind that classical music was playing. His eyes searched for the source of the music. There, in the center of the large, open space stood an enormous Christmas tree with all the trimmings. Beside it, a man sat at a black lacquer baby grand piano, playing his heart out. Beckett grunted. Except for himself, the receptionist, and a security guard, the space was empty. Such a waste of resources.

The familiar scent of floor cleaner assaulted his nose, bringing back a trove of memories. How many times had he rushed across a polished floor identical to this one, donning a custom suit and black leather shoes, offering glib comments to the security guys as he rushed to catch an elevator? He'd felt invincible then, ready to make his mark on the world. How naïve he was. He swallowed. "I'm here to see Houston Thomas." He rested his hands on the top of the booth, trying to appear more composed than he felt. Everything in him wanted to flee this place, forget that Houston Thomas had ever shown up at the station this morning.

"Your name?"

"Beckett Bradshaw."

"Yes." For the first time, the woman smiled like he'd suddenly met with her approval. "Mr. Thomas is expecting you." She pointed. "Take the elevator up to the tenth floor. Mr. Thomas will be waiting for you."

"Thanks," he clipped.

The first thing Beckett saw when the elevator opened was Houston, who offered a brief nod. "I'm glad you came."

Not knowing how to answer, Beckett only nodded.

Houston shuffled down the hall, getting a few steps away before he beckoned for Beckett to follow. "This way."

As nice as the foyer was, the executive suites were even statelier with the patterned ruby-red wallpaper-covered walls and handsome cherry crown molding. The hall opened to a large sitting area that boasted soft camel leather couches and high-back chairs. Spacious offices surrounded the perimeter of the area. A few of the doors were open, and Beckett could tell they were occupied. Again, he wondered what this was about.

Houston stepped through the door on their left. For a second, Beckett hesitated, then went in behind him. Houston sat down behind the desk and motioned. "Have a seat."

Beckett's pulse was thrashing a fast beat against his neck. He was hot all over except for his hands, which were ice cold. As inconspicuously as he could, he took in a breath, willing himself to get a grip. PTSD was a beast. Never would Beckett have imagined that it would be so difficult to come back to an office building. Well, it wasn't just the office, but also fear of what Houston had to tell him.

Houston sat back in his chair and folded his legs, adjusting his crease as he'd done at the station. "I'm sure you're wondering why I asked you to come here today."

"Yes." His heart pounded out a frenzied beat like a basketball being dribbled across the court. He was ready for the man to just come out with it. *Geez.* How much longer was he going to draw this out?

"According to a report generated this morning, McQueen Capital Group has an estimated value of 2.2 billion dollars."

"What does that have to do with me?"

Houston held up a hand. "Hold your horses. I'm about to tell you. Milton McQueen was the founder of the company. He placed all the assets and properties of the capital group into a living trust. He was the trustee. Upon Milton's death, I became the successor trustee. It therefore becomes my responsibility to inform you that you are the designated beneficiary of the living trust."

"Huh?" A laugh rumbled in Beckett's throat. "Is this some kind of joke?" He kept waiting for Houston to break into a smile and point a finger saying, *Gotcha!* When that didn't happen, Beckett coughed, scooting forward. "There must be some mistake."

Houston didn't even blink. "I assure you, there's no mistake."

A fist closed around Beckett's throat as panic engulfed him. For a second, he couldn't breathe. "No, that's not possible. I didn't even know Milton McQueen."

Alarm streaked through Houston's eyes. "Are you okay?"

Beckett coughed again, trying to take in a breath.

Houston pushed a button. "Teresa, can I get a glass of water, please? Now!" The intercom clicked off.

This couldn't be happening. A wave of dizziness rolled over Beckett as he tried to grasp what was happening. He didn't want a company, the high-rise building, or the fancy furniture!

Two seconds later, a woman hurried in holding a glass of water. She tried to hand it to Houston, but he pointed to Beckett who took the glass and chugged down the whole of the water in three swallows. "Thank you," he breathed, handing it back.

The woman looked at Houston. "Will there be anything else, Mr. Thomas?"

"Thank you," he drawled. "That'll do for now. Close the door when you leave, would ya?"

"Sure," she said, doing as instructed.

"Are you all right?" Houston asked.

Beckett nodded, noting the sympathetic expression on the older man's face. "Why would Milton McQueen draft a will, leaving everything to me?"

Houston held up a finger. "Not a will, but a living trust."

"Okay, is there a difference?"

"A very significant difference. A living trust remains private as opposed to a will, which is public. There won't be any court dates, etc. Everything will transfer to you immediately."

Beckett had the feeling of the floor falling out from underneath him as he gripped the arms of the chair. "I don't want it. Any of it."

Houston sat back in his chair. "Milton was afraid you'd say that."

"You keep acting like Milton knew me, but I never met him. I tell you, this is a mistake. Maybe he meant to leave everything to another guy named Beckett Bradshaw."

Houston laughed, stroking the sides of his mustache. "You have met Milton, on several occasions. You probably just didn't realize who he was."

He turned to the credenza behind his chair and reached for a framed photo, handing it to Beckett.

Beckett went bug-eyed. "That's Steve from the park."

"See, I told you. You did know Milton."

"No, his name was Steve." He heard a chortle, saw the smirk on Houston's face. "Steve was really Milton?" This was crazy. About a year after he came off the streets, before he became a firefighter, he worked as a server in a restaurant while trying to plan his future. He'd spent a lot of time at a park near the restaurant. It was there where he met Steve. Their conversation had been mostly superficial. "I don't understand what's happening here." He handed the photo back to Houston.

"Milton followed your career. He told me how you saved that little girl from a fire last year."

"Yeah, but that's just part of the job description. Any other fire-fighter would've done the same." Beckett and the crew had responded to a fire in an apartment complex. They'd searched the units and thought everyone had been removed. Then, a frantic woman came running up to Beckett, saying her daughter was still inside on the third floor, apartment 312. Without a second thought, Beckett rushed back into the complex and rescued the girl. The media got wind of the story, touting him as a hero.

Houston tipped his head thoughtfully. "But your colleagues didn't rescue the girl. You did."

Beckett rubbed his jaw. "Yes, because I happened to be the one the woman approached." He paused. "At any rate, that's not a valid reason for leaving a person your fortune. Doesn't Milton have any relatives?"

"Yes, I was just getting to that. Milton had a son, daughter, and granddaughter."

"All right. There ya go. Let them have it." He stood. "I have all that I need. I'm happy with my life."

Houston chuckled dryly. "Just like that, you're giving it all up?"

"How can I give up something that I never had?"

"Sit back down. Please. Just hear me out."

Beckett blew out a breath. His teeth ground together as he leveled a glare at Houston. "All right. Spill it. You've got thirty seconds before I'm out of here."

"Milton wanted his company and assets to go to someone who would manage them responsibly."

A hysterical laugh bubbled in Beckett's throat. "Then you've definitely got the wrong man. The last time people trusted me with their money, well, it didn't go very well. If Milton knew my history, then he wouldn't have picked me."

"He knew everything about you."

Beckett was at a loss for words as he raked a hand through his hair.

"Milton knew exactly what he was doing," Houston asserted.

"What about his kids? Did he just cut them off cold turkey?"

"No, he gave them each a sizable inheritance—five hundred million dollars." Houston gave him a significant look. "Here's the clincher. There's a no contest clause written into the trust."

"What does that mean?" A headache was making a punching bag out of Beckett's forehead. Maybe this was all some crazy dream ... or nightmare. In another life, he might've thought it was a dream come true to inherit a fortune, but not with his past. *All that glitters is not gold.* Beckett had the urge to laugh uncontrollably. That's what the Fruitcake Lady told him. Was that what she meant? How in the heck did she know this was going to happen to him? Yes, this had to be a dream. Hopefully, he'd wake up soon.

"It means that if any of the relatives contest the trust ... if they lose in court, they'll forfeit their inheritance."

"What provision did Milton make in the event that I refuse to accept the inheritance?"

"He didn't. He was sure you'd take it."

"But you said Milton knew I wouldn't be pleased about it."

"That's right."

"And yet, he still thought I'd eventually go along with it?"

A sly smile spread over Houston's lips, the tips of his mustache turning up. "Yep."

Beckett scrunched his brows. "Why?"

"I guess it'll all eventually come out in the wash. Until then, the best thing you can do is not make any rash decisions." He propped his elbows on his desk, his fingers forming a triangle. "Think of all the people you could help."

The warm glow that spread through Beckett caught him completely off guard. Hadn't he just thought about the waste of the piano player and the lavish executive suites? He, of all people, knew the suffering of the homeless. Could he really turn his back on these resources without at least attempting to help others?

Houston's face lit up. "Ah, I see you're thinking about it. That's good." He stood and came around the desk. "Come on. I'll introduce you to the executive team members."

"I didn't say I was going along with this," Beckett countered, not liking how he was being corralled.

"I know, but you're here. It's as good of a time as any to meet everyone. Come on now," he urged. "Stand up."

Beckett got to his feet. He couldn't believe this was happening. What was he supposed to do with a real estate company worth 2.2 billion dollars? That kind of wealth was unprecedented, staggering. Like a lamb going to the slaughter, he followed Houston to the office next door. Houston rapped his knuckles a couple times on the door before opening it.

A thin-faced man with sharp features looked up from his computer.

"Hey, Ted," Houston said pleasantly. "There's someone here I want you to meet." Houston turned to Beckett. "Ted is Milton's oldest child and the CEO of McQueen Capital Group."

Ted stood, irritation clouding his features over being interrupted. "What is this?" he asked suspiciously.

Maybe it was an unfair assessment, but Beckett took an instant dislike to Ted. He represented everything in his former profession that Beckett had gladly left behind.

Houston's eyes lit with amusement. "Ted. Meet Beckett Bradshaw ... the beneficiary of the trust."

Talk about walking in and pulling the pin on the grenade! In another situation, Ted's reaction would've been comical. However, Beckett was also peeved that Houston was spilling the beans so brashly. "What're you doing?" he muttered.

"Well, I reckon you can pick at the Band-aid all day long or just rip the dang thing off," Houston mused.

Ted's face turned blood red. "This is outrageous!" His voice rose, the veins in his neck popping like ropes. "Do you really expect me to believe my dad named some stranger the beneficiary of his trust?"

"Yep," Houston said proudly.

"W—what?" Ted's jaw went slack and Beckett noticed his hands started to shake. A second later, he threw his hands in the air, his venom aimed at Beckett. "Who is this Bozo, anyway?"

Beckett straightened to his full height. "The name's Beckett Bradshaw." He thrust out his hand, looking Ted in the eye. "Nice to meet you."

Ted grated out a shrill laugh, looking in disdain at Beckett's outstretched hand.

"I'd shake the man's hand, Ted. He's now your new boss," Houston said amiably.

"No!" Ted roared. "I won't allow this!"

Houston's eyebrows shot up. "You need to get control of yourself," he warned. "It won't do any of us any good if you cause a ruckus."

Ted grunted, shooting Houston a venomous look. "You think you're so superior, don't you, old man? Working your little schemes. You're the reason Dad and I didn't get along."

"Nope, that had nothing to do with me, Ted. You did that all on your own, because of your selfishness and greed. Milton gave you and Libby plenty of opportunities to change. When you didn't, he made other plans." He looked at Beckett.

Beckett dropped his hand to his side. Everything felt surreal. Sure, his first impression of Ted wasn't great, but he could hardly blame the guy for being upset. Houston seemed a little too happy to rub Ted's nose in it. Beckett figured there was some bad blood between the two. He wasn't sure what he thought about Houston, but he liked him better than Ted.

"Libby and Bill won't stand for it either!" There was a crazed look in Ted's eyes.

"Libby is Ted's sister. Bill is Libby's husband and the CFO of McQueen Capital Group," Houston explained. He stroked his mustache looking thoughtful. "Well, Ted, I reckon y'all will have to 'stand for it'. Milton put in a no contest clause. You fight it in court and lose..." He let out a low chuckle. "Well, then you forfeit every dime of your inheritance." He shoved his hands into his pockets, rocking forward on his boots. "The trust is ironclad, I guarantee you that. I drafted it myself. Oh, and in case you think you wanna go for the Milton not being of sound mind angle, you should know that he had psychiatric evaluations by a dozen renown psychiatrists."

Ted's face had turned an ugly purple as he balled his fists. Beckett feared he might have a heart attack or aneurysm. It would be the ultimate irony to have to jump into medic mode and try to save the man's life.

Ted glared at Beckett, the words dripping like poison from his mouth. "Let me guess, you're some real estate guru, a shiny new toy that caught my dad's eye."

Beckett glanced at Houston, caught the amused flicker in the older man's eyes. It kindled something inside Beckett, bringing with it an ember of fire in his belly from his previous life. "Actually," he said, straight-faced, "I'm a firefighter."

Ted made a gurgling sound like he was choking. "You've got to be kidding!"

Houston scratched his head, mirth dancing in his eyes. "Naw, I can attest to the fact that Beckett is indeed a firefighter. I visited him at his station this morning."

"What a freak show!" He pointed at Houston. "You won't get away with this, old man!" Ted seethed, storming out.

Houston tipped his head and shrugged. "Well, that went better than expected," he said cheerfully.

A humorless laugh rumbled in Beckett's throat. Houston was either cool as a cucumber or putting on one heck of a show. "I don't know what your definition of good is, but that wasn't mine." He tightened his jaw. "Further, I don't appreciate you using me as leverage against Ted to settle some past score."

"That's not how it went down at all, Beckett," Houston said conversationally. He paused, his next words holding significance. "If you're gonna have any hope of taking charge of the mule, you've gotta show a firm hand. Remember that."

Beckett didn't want to show anything right now. He rubbed a hand across his aching forehead, longing to get out of this place and go somewhere quiet where he could process everything. Life had thrown him a doozy of a curve ball this time—the enticement of riches at the risk of losing himself down the dark, slippery path of his demons. Did he really have it in him to go down this road again? He couldn't believe he was thinking this, but he was actually tempted to give it a shot. Obviously, Milton McQueen had seen something in him. The last time, he'd been the underdog, trying to prove himself. Now, he was holding all the power. It boggled his mind to think someone he hardly knew would trust him enough to leave him his fortune.

Houston put an arm around his shoulder. "Come on, I'll introduce you to a couple more people."

CHAPTER 10

The next office door was open. Houston strode in with Beckett close behind. From the minute they entered the room, Beckett could tell from the wary expression of the man sitting behind the desk that he'd heard Ted's outburst. "Bill," Houston said ceremoniously with a flourish of his hand. "This is Beckett Bradshaw, Milton's designated beneficiary to his living trust and the new owner of McQueen Capital Group."

The man's ruddy complexion turned as red as his hair as he stood and gave Beckett a limp handshake.

"I know this is a lot to take in," Houston continued, "but it's how Milton wanted it."

Bill had a deer in the headlights look. "Does Libby know?"

"Not yet, but I'm sure you'll do the honor," Houston said.

"Of course," he uttered. He looked at Beckett. "Do you even know anything about commercial real estate?" His voice was laced with condescension.

Before Beckett could answer, Houston piped in, "If he doesn't, he can learn. You did," he added dourly.

Bill jerked, his eyes hardening with resentment.

"Sorry to interrupt you," Houston said, signaling the end of the conversation. It was impressive, how Houston navigated effortlessly through all the volatile personalities, the helm of a boat cutting swiftly through treacherous waters.

"Uh, okay," Bill stuttered.

"Nice meeting you," Beckett said, holding the heavyset man's eyes. Bill seemed okay. He'd obviously gotten the job as CFO because he was married to Libby, but how was his job performance? That was the determining factor, the one Beckett would be examining. Well, that is, if he accepted the inheritance.

"Yeah," Bill mumbled, looking down.

When they got back out to the sitting area, Houston smiled. "See, that wasn't so bad. Once the dust settles, everything will be fine."

Beckett highly doubted that.

"The next person I want you to meet is Wesley Howard, the marketing director." Houston pointed. "This way."

As they entered Wesley's office, the man stood, a ready smile on his face as he extended his hand, giving Beckett's a hearty shake. "I hear congratulations are in order."

Houston looked puzzled. "How did you know?"

"Ted told me, a few minutes ago."

"Ah, Ted's been busy, I see."

Beckett took an assessment of Wesley. He appeared to be in his early thirties with wavy blonde hair and in-your-face good looks. Beckett's first impression of Wesley was that he was a little too polished and accommodating, like he was trying to kiss up to the new boss. He'd seen Wesley's type too many times to count—shake with one hand while stabbing you in the back with the other. Instantly, Beckett felt guilty for judging Wesley so harshly. He didn't even know the man. He needed to give him a chance, rather than lumping him in with past stereotypes.

Houston's phone rang. He fished it out of his pocket. "I'd better get this." He held up a finger. "Excuse me, gentlemen."

An awkward silence stretched between Beckett and Wesley. "Have a seat," Wesley said.

Beckett sat down.

Wesley sat back in his chair, lacing his fingers together. "So, you're the fireman."

Something about the way Wesley delivered the statement sat wrong with Beckett. "Yes, I am," he said proudly.

"You must be on top of the world right now." Wesley snorted a derisive chuckle. "One day you're a regular, blue-collar guy, out fighting fires and saving the neighborhood. The next, you're named the beneficiary of a multi-billion-dollar trust. You won the jackpot, not to mention the girl."

Beckett's breath froze as he tipped his head. "What did you say?"

All pretense of friendliness vanished as a scornful smile twisted over Wesley's lips. "I wondered what Ava saw in you."

Beckett punched out a startled breath. "What're you talking about?" he growled, scooting to the edge of his seat.

"Oh, you didn't know?" Wesley laughed. "Let me guess, you thought Ava loved you." He shook his head in mock sympathy.

Beckett felt like he was being swept down a raging river, trying to keep his mouth and nose above water. "What does Ava have to do with any of this?" His pulse throbbed out a hard, fast beat against his temples.

Wesley shook his head, his voice taking on the taunting edge of a tiger toying with its prey. "The girl's good, I'll give her that."

Beckett's blood boiled. "You'd better explain yourself right now before I jump across the desk and rip that smirk off your face!"

"Ava is Milton McQueen's granddaughter ... and my fiancée," Wesley added triumphantly. "You probably didn't connect the two because Ava goes by her mother's maiden name instead of *McQueen*." He held up his phone, showing Beckett his screensaver—a picture of Wesley and Ava together. Wesley's arm was slung around Ava's shoulders, and she was looking at him with adoring eyes.

The air left Beckett's lungs as the room began to spin. Wesley's voice seemed like it was coming from far away.

"It's a hard break, man," Wesley added.

All this time, Ava had been playing him. No wonder she didn't want him to know where she lived.

Wesley grunted. "Ava's the smart one in the bunch. Ted will kick and scream and Libby will pout, but Ava ..." a look of admiration came over Wesley, along with a cruel smile "... Ava went with the love con. Brilliant! The one who controls you, controls the trust."

Somehow, Beckett managed to get to his feet as he stumbled out of the office. He caught sight of Houston out of the corner of his eye. The older man pulled the phone away from his ear, his features drooping into a frown. "What's going on?"

Beckett kept on moving. As he exited the building, Ava came running up. When she saw him, she stopped in her tracks, her face draining. "I'm sorry." Tears rose in her eyes. "I wanted to be here when Houston told you." She barked out a laugh. "I didn't realize Houston was meeting with you until the last minute. Then, I got a speeding ticket on the way over."

Every muscle in Beckett's body quivered, and it was all he could do to control his voice as he ground out the words. "How could you? I trusted you!" His voice was like thunder, his anguish rising in his chest like a hideous, black mountain. He looked at the woman he thought he was falling in love with. Even with her pinched expression and pale face, she was exquisite—a beautiful Jezebel who'd murmured sweet lies into his ear to manipulate him. Her golden hair still called to him, making him want to run his fingers through it. Her crystal eyes were regretful, worried as they sought his. "I wanted to tell you the truth." Her voice was persuasively soft.

How easy it would be to take her into his arms, forget that she'd used him.

"What truth is that?" he barked, heat combusting through him. "That you used me!"

She rocked back. "No, I never used you."

He snarled out a laugh. "Of course you did. You were bitter because your grandfather named me as beneficiary of his living trust. You thought if you could trick me into falling in love with you that you'd have complete control."

Her lower lip trembled, eyes filling with panic. "No, that's not true. I would never do that. I wanted to tell you the truth, planned to be here when Houston met with you so I could tell you. My grandfather's instructions were very clear and precise, Houston was the one who was supposed to deliver the news. I didn't want to break protocol and run the risk of messing anything up."

He grunted. "That was mighty convenient, huh?" Something else occurred to him. "No wonder you didn't seem all that surprised when I told you about my past." He got up in her face, his voice escalating. "You already knew, didn't you?"

"Yes," she croaked, a tear running down her cheek. "You've got to believe me. I would never do anything to hurt you. I'm falling in love with you."

The words he most wanted to hear. Now, they were a cruel mockery. His head was on fire. He threw up his hands, pushing out a hard laugh. "I find that hard to believe!"

"Why's that?"

"Must I spell it out? You're engaged to another man!"

An incredulous laugh rumbled in her throat. "What?"

He held up a hand. "Don't try to deny it," he lashed out. "I saw the picture of you and Wesley." His insides were being gutted.

"I don't know how in the heck you got that idea, but you're dead wrong."

She was convincing with the sparks shooting from her eyes, nostrils flaring. He wanted to believe her, but the proof of her treachery was plain as day. There was a two billion-dollar trust on the line and Beckett got in the way. Rage tightened his chest, making it hard to breathe.

She touched his arm. "Let's go inside, and I'll explain everything to you. Please."

"You must think I'm stupid." He laughed, shaking his head. "I guess I am stupid. I thought I was in love with you." He jerked his arm out of her grasp. The fingers of despair clutched the base of his skull. "No!" He had to get away. "Don't ever contact me again!"

He pushed past her.

"Beckett," she screamed, her voice shrill. "Hear me out! Please!"

Tears wet his eyes as he swallowed down the despair in his throat. His feet picked up the pace and then he was running.

For the first time in years, all he could think was how badly he needed a drink.

Beckett sat slumped over the edge of the bar, looking down into the shot glass filled with clear liquid. All he had to do to end the pain was bring the glass to his lips, tip it up, and swallow. Ava had been calling repeatedly, had left over a dozen texts, telling him that they needed to talk. As far as Beckett was concerned, there was nothing left to say. He'd also missed a few calls from Jazzie, wondering why he'd not come to pick her up.

His heart tugged. *Jazzie!* If he threw in the towel and started drinking again, Jazzie would be the one who got hurt the most.

"That's right, she would be hurt the most."

He jumped, startled that the woman beside him had spoken. He turned to look at her. For a second, he thought his eyes were deceiving him. He blinked, then looked again. His weary mind was imagining things. Maybe his brain was tricking him. He'd been sitting here for hours, staring into the liquid. Before that, he'd gotten in his truck and drove aimlessly before finally ending up at a bar. Maybe he was in a drunken state, hallucinating. "You're the Fruitcake Lady," he uttered. She was wearing the same brown cape he remembered. Her eyes twinkled as she smiled, the leathery wrinkles deepening.

"Yes."

"Well, your prophecy of me finding love by Christmas came true." His stomach clenched as he let out an acerbic laugh "Of course, I lost it just as quickly. You forgot to add that part in."

She dipped her head in a thoughtful pose. "I guess that depends on your definition of *lost*."

He picked up the glass, swirling the liquid. One little drink, that's all he needed to take the edge off.

"It never stops with one," the woman countered in a scratchy voice.

He sat the glass down with an audible plunk. "How do you keep doing that? Are you clairvoyant or something?" he mumbled.

Amusement lit her eyes. "Something like that." Her tone grew speculative. "You know, earlier, your thoughts were right on track. You could do a lot of good with the inheritance."

He jerked. "How?" he sputtered. He grunted, rubbing his jaw. "None of that matters anymore. I'm not accepting it."

He expected her to offer a response, but she just sat there, staring at him with those beady eyes. He swore she could see straight into his soul. "What?" he barked insolently. He bunched his brows, his fingers curling around the glass.

"It was her choice."

"What?" he barked.

She pointed. "Who's that?"

He turned to look. "Who're you pointing to?"

In a swift movement, belying her age, she snatched the glass from his hands and downed the liquid.

"Hey!" Beckett countered.

She shuddered, making a face. "That has got to be the nastiest stuff I've ever tasted."

"You can't just take someone's drink!"

Her thin lips stretched into a smile that seemed to fall into the back of her mouth. "Now, the temptation's gone," she said glibly.

A laugh bubbled in Beckett's throat. Surprisingly, he felt relieved.

"See." She tapped his arm. "You don't need that anymore. You're a changed man."

His brain worked trying to unearth a forgotten memory. It was right there on the edge of his mind. For the life of him, he couldn't quite get to it. He turned to her, studying her stringy tufts of cotton-white hair, lined face, and mismatched clothing swallowing her tiny frame. "We've met before."

She tipped a half smile, speaking to him in a slow, precise

cadence like she was talking to a child. "Yes, at the fire station and when you helped me move into my house."

"Ah, but I went to the house we helped you move into, there was another family living there who said they'd been there for two years and had never heard of you."

A giddy laugh escaped her lips. "Oops," she quipped, touching her mouth.

"I mean we met before that." He rubbed his forehead. "At least I think we have." Maybe he was losing it.

She let out a labored sigh. "No, you're not losing it. We have, sort of, met before. It's not important," she said hastily.

"But—"

"But, you need to listen to me," she said, her voice ringing with authority.

Beckett marveled at how he felt compelled to listen to her. There was an inherent strength to the Yoda-like woman that commanded respect.

"It was Ava's choice to make you the beneficiary of her grandfather's trust."

He jerked, his breath coming out in a loud gasp. "H—how do you know about Ava?" Was the woman telling the truth?

"Deep down, you already know that I am," she countered. "Ava's grandfather would've left everything to her, had she desired it. Ava wanted you to have it because she knew you would be a wise steward." She gave him a motherly smile. "All that glitters is not gold."

Beckett's mind raced as he tried to make sense of what was happening.

"Search your heart. Find the strength to forgive yourself for your past mistakes. Don't be afraid to ask God for help. He doesn't keep score of the blessings He gives you." She stood.

His mind was on fire. If it was Ava's choice to leave Beckett the inheritance that could mean only one thing—that she really was falling for him.

The woman's eyes glittered with an ancient mirth that seemed to defy time and space. "Now you're on the right track."

He caught hold of her cape. "W—who are you?"

She scrunched her face, her wrinkles caving in on one another, shriveling it like a raisin. He held his breath as she peered into his eyes. Then she pushed a bony finger into his chest. "That's not what you should be asking."

"Huh?"

The corners of her lips tipped into a shrewd smile. "The question you should be asking is, *Who are you?*" She grew pensive, holding up a gnarled finger. "What kind of man is Beckett Bradshaw?" Pulling her cape tighter around her stooped shoulders, she turned and hobbled away.

Beckett reached in his wallet and slapped down a ten-dollar bill for the drink. He couldn't let the woman get away, not without finding out who she was and how she knew so much about him.

He hurried after her. When he stepped outside the bar, he scoured the surrounding area.

The woman was nowhere to be found.

CHAPTER 11

Beckett sat in his truck, staring aimlessly at the swirling snowflakes colliding with the windshield and running down the glass in watery ribbons. If all that the woman had said was true ... Tears pressed against his eyes. She'd admonished him to pray, to ask for the things he needed most. He needed Ava, needed the strength to take hold of this new responsibility. At the bar, he'd sat for hours staring into the abyss, the need for alcohol almost unbearable. And yet, somehow, he'd not succumbed to temptation.

He laughed bringing his fist to his mouth. Of course, it helped that the little, old lady drank it. *It's time,* his heart whispered. *Time to put away the old and embrace the new.* Hot tears spilled down his cheeks as he closed his eyes and bowed his head, opening his heart in prayer.

An hour later, Beckett felt like a heavy weight had been lifted from his chest as he pulled into his driveway and turned off the engine. Had it not been so late, Beckett would've called Ava to work things out. He still wasn't pleased that she'd withheld the truth from him, pretended that their first meeting was happenstance. But, he couldn't deny his feelings for her. The snow was coming down harder. He got out of his truck and tucked his chin into his neck as he

walked briskly to the entrance of his apartment. He climbed the stairs
to his loft on the second floor. As he stepped inside the door, he
dusted the snow from his hair and removed his coat, tossing it on a
nearby chair. He was physically exhausted, but too keyed up to sleep.

He was headed to the kitchen to grab a bottle of water out of the
fridge when he caught movement in his peripheral vision. He spun
around and saw a man rushing towards him—blonde hair, an expression of pure hatred. Hot prickles of surprise jolted through Beckett
like an electrical charge as his mind connected the person with the
face. "Wesley?"

"Lights out, wonder boy," Wesley said maliciously, swinging a bat.

Beckett held up his hands in defense, heard a loud pop at the
same instant a blinding pain shot through his head. He staggered and
fell, going deadly still.

Hunger gnawed at Beckett's gut, his footsteps heavy as he trudged
through the wet snow. He was again homeless, Jazzie's pleading
expression searing through his mind. He'd just left the shelter where
Jazzie had begged him to come home, but he couldn't. His weak-
nesses bound him with bands of steel, impossible to break through. A
picture of Ava flashed through his mind. With it came an overwhelming feeling of longing and an urgency to get to her.

The hunger persisted, nipping at his insides like a ruthless dog.
No, he couldn't be hungry. He was rich beyond his wildest dreams. *All
that glitters is not gold.* The money meant nothing in comparison to his
relationships. Beckett thought of Jazzie, his parents and siblings, Ava.
All thoughts kept going back to Ava, the moon pulling the tides.

He was on the train, wrapped in the suffocating blanket of his
guilt. A UTA transit officer boarded the train. Beckett tensed,
wondering if he'd be thrown off for not having a ticket. Wait a
minute! Was this a dream? He'd lived this before. The officer was
coming his direction, methodically checking all the passengers' tickets. The officer stopped by the woman sitting directly in front of

Beckett. Beckett looked, then looked again. Brown cloak, snow-white hair, stooped shoulders. The woman turned so that he caught a glimpse of her face.

He flinched. "It's you!" Why was the Fruitcake Lady on the train? She was arguing with the UTA officer, causing a scene. The officer put her in cuffs, was about to haul her off. She caught Beckett's eye and smiled, wide-cheeked, her mouth falling back into her face as it had at the bar.

"You caused a distraction to keep me from getting thrown off the train. Why?"

The scene shifted, and he was once again trudging through the snow. He was encapsulated in the isolation of the deserted rural road. No, he wasn't alone. Someone else was here. He saw the headlights and the car in the snow. He felt like he was separated from himself, watching a story unfold as he went to investigate, then came across the woman. She reached for his hand, begging him to stay with her. He felt more than heard the thoughts in his head, could tell how hard it was for him to break through his protective shell of isolation. For so long he'd kept himself quarantined from other people. He was no longer Beckett Bradshaw, a productive citizen, but a faceless vagrant scavenging the streets to survive. Still, something inside him whispered that he couldn't leave the woman. He warred with himself, that epic battle of right and wrong waging, his need to help another human being winning out in the end.

Beckett's body convulsed as he coughed in acrid smoke. Hands shook his arms.

"Wake up!" a scratchy voice ordered.

He opened his eyes and strained to see. Smoke burned his eyes. It only took a second for his mind to process what was happening. He was in a fire! He felt his clothes, his hands frantically patting down his torso, wondering why he wasn't in uniform. Where was the crew?

"You have to get out!"

He forced his brain to focus on the blurry face hovering over him. Old with loose wrinkles. "It's you again. The Fruitcake La—" The words choked in his throat as he coughed. His chest hurt from the smoke. Pain throbbed through his head. He touched the back of it, surprised to find it sticky and wet.

The old woman tugged at his arm. "Get moving! You haven't got much time."

He groaned as he sat up, then doubled over coughing. His head swam as the woman shoved him. Instinct took over as he lifted the bottom of his shirt to his mouth and crawled toward the stairs. *Stand up and you're dead. Stay low and go!* The heat was blistering, causing rivulets of sweat to drip from his forehead. His eyeballs felt like they were burning through to the sockets as he strained to see through the smoke. Normally, Beckett and his crew would try to find the source of the fire and contain it. Then, they'd methodically check the structure, room by room, for victims. In this case, he was the victim. He heard a cracking sound as the far end of the room caved in. He had to get out! Getting to his feet, he went down the stairs. When he got to the bottom, he kicked open the door, practically falling out of it into the cold, night air. Large snowflakes swirled around him as he got to his feet and turned to face his building, clutching his chest. Smoke billowed from the roof. Where was the woman? Had she gotten out?

It went through his mind that every worldly possession he owned was in that building. He heard the squeal of the fire engine siren, briefly wondered which shift was working tonight, as he staggered onto the snowy grass and collapsed.

CHAPTER 12

The persistent ringing of Ava's phone jolted her out of her sleep. She groaned as she reached for the phone. "Hello." Her voice was groggy, and she felt like she'd been hit by a truck. She'd been so distraught over Beckett, afraid that he'd never speak to her again, that she'd not gotten to sleep until two a.m. Her mind kept rolling everything around, making her feel more and more guilty for not telling Beckett the truth straight out. Hang the conditions of the trust! Ava should've been the one to tell him. She was still peeved at Houston for going through with it, even when she asked him to wait.

No hello or *good morning*. "Have you seen the local news?" Houston asked bluntly.

She raked her hair away from her forehead, exhaling a dry laugh. "Sure, I've been up since five a.m. watching it," she said sarcastically.

In characteristic Houston form, he completely ignored her comment. "Beckett's loft apartment caught on fire last night."

She sat up, all trace of sleep vanishing as she tightened her grip on the phone. "Is he okay? What happened?" She held her breath, awaiting his answer, tears springing to her eyes.

"He's been rushed to the hospital."

She jumped out of bed, her heart thumping. "Oh, no! Is he going to be okay?"

"That's all I know at this point. In fact, I wouldn't have known anything at all had I not been watching the 5 a.m. news this morning and recognized Beckett's building."

Ava's mind raced. How could this be happening? Ava had lost everyone else in the world she cared about. She couldn't lose Beckett too! Rushing to her closet, she began grabbing clothes to throw on.

"Ava?"

"Yeah?" she said hurriedly.

"There's more."

"What?" Her breath caught as she braced herself.

"Wesley was arrested for arson and attempted murder."

She gulped in a loud breath, her hand going over her chest. "Are you sure?" A wave of dizziness assaulted her. "Why would Wesley do such a thing?" she breathed, white-hot anger shooting through her.

"Probably to eliminate the competition," Houston said dryly. "Wesley's got it bad for you. I'm sure he thought with Beckett out of the picture, you'd turn to him. In the end, he could get you and the trust."

Chill bumps rose over Ava's arms. She'd felt it that night—the feeling of alarm that something wasn't right with Wesley. Her stomach knotted. She had to get to Beckett. *Please let him be okay*, she prayed. "Which hospital is Beckett in?"

"St. John's."

Ava's mind was spinning so fast she couldn't think straight. She pulled on a pair of jeans. "Hang on a sec." She pulled the phone away from her ear and slipped on a sweatshirt. "How do the authorities know it was Wesley?"

Houston let out a throaty chuckle. "That's the strangest part about this whole thing. Evidently, as Wesley was going to his car to flee the scene, he found an old woman bashing out his headlights with a crowbar. She'd already banged the side of his car with a shopping cart a few times. Wesley tried to stop her, but the woman attacked him, making such a ruckus that it woke the neighbors. A few minutes later, one of them came out and started filming. Then he smelled smoke, realized Beckett's place was on fire and called 911. Had the old woman not been there, Wesley might've gotten away with it."

Her shoes now on, Ava grabbed her purse and keys. She was almost to the garage when she thought of something else—the thing she'd been wanting to show Beckett for a long time. Jogging back to her bedroom closet, she used the wooden stepladder to reach the top shelf, pulling down a box. She ripped off the packing tape, opened the box, and pulled out the item, clutching it in her arms as she darted out the door.

A nurse approached Beckett's bed, giving him a sympathetic look. "On a scale from one to ten, what's your pain level right now?"

"About a five." He winced, fighting the urge to touch the base of his skull. A dull pain shot through his head with every beat of his pulse, and his eyes were still burning. He coughed hoarsely, his hand cradling his chest.

The nurse pushed a needle into the IV stream. "This will help take the edge off."

"Morphine?" he asked.

"Yep. Giving you ten more."

"What's the plan from here on?" Beckett wanted to leave the hospital as soon as possible.

"The doctor's still waiting to get the results of the CT-scan. Once he has those, he can determine if you have a fracture or any internal bleeding. All of those factors will determine the length of your stay."

He let out a long breath, fingering the blanket. "Thanks," he mumbled. The hospital was not where he wanted to be three days before Christmas. As soon as Beckett had gotten assigned a hospital room, he used the hospital phone to call his parents. His mother had burst into tears. Beckett had to keep reassuring her that he would be okay. Unfortunately, he wasn't sure how badly the loft was burned.

He suspected it would be a total loss with the roof caving in the way
it had.

"What was the cause of the fire," his dad wanted to know, "faulty
wiring?"

Beckett had tiptoed around the subject the best he could, saying
he'd explain everything in person when they arrived at the hospital.
His parents would flip when they realized all that had happened.
Better to break it to them gently. Next, he called Jazzie, apologizing
for not calling her yesterday or showing up to go shopping. He told
her about the fire and his, hopefully short, hospital stay. Jazzie had
also started crying. Briefly, he spoke to Melinda who assured Beckett
that she'd bring Jazzie to the hospital later this afternoon. The fire
crew was coming too. One by one, they'd called to check on him the
minute they heard.

More than anything, Beckett wanted to speak to Ava. He didn't
have her number memorized. He grunted. He didn't even have a cell
phone or access to a computer. All he could do was sit here and wait
for the doctor to get the scan results.

He relaxed against the pillow, staring unseeingly at the sitcom on
the TV. His mind raced a mile a minute as he replayed the strange
events that had come at him in such a short period of time. He'd
returned home from the bar, pondering over his strange meeting
with the Fruitcake Lady and how she'd helped him clarify things in
his mind. She'd prompted him to pray. It was the prayer that helped
restore a sense of peace. He got the direct impression that the lady
was right—God wasn't keeping score of the blessings. His love was
endless. All this time, He'd been standing there, waiting for Beckett
to let Him fully back into his life.

Beckett was starting to feel excitement over his inheritance,
thinking of the many ways he could put it to good use. He decided
that he could oversee the business and keep his job as a firefighter.
With his two-day-on and four-day-off work schedule, it was doable.
Beckett had found himself again in the camaraderie of the crew and
responsibilities of the job, and he wasn't about to give that up.

Also, he'd been thinking how he wanted to talk to Ava. Not just talk. He wanted to pull her into his arms and kiss her for the duration of a thousand lifetimes. Then, Wesley attacked with the bat and set his loft on fire. He clutched the blanket. The Fruitcake Lady had come to him, helped him get out of the fire. Had she not been there ... A shudder ran down his spine. He wouldn't be here right now.

Beckett remembered everything he'd dreamt while unconscious. The Fruitcake Lady had been there too, keeping him from getting thrown off the train. The question was—Why? Why did she keep popping in and out of his life? There was no way the woman could've followed him home from the bar and gotten into his loft to help him escape. No surprise, none of the other firefighters who responded to the call saw her. Beckett had never given much thought to guardian angels, but now he was starting to suspect that maybe the Fruitcake Lady was one.

The icing on the cake was what the police officer had told him when he came to the hospital to get a statement from Beckett. Wesley Howard had been taken into custody. The officer related how Wesley had an altercation with a homeless lady. The event was captured on video by Beckett's neighbors, placing Wesley at the scene of the crime. That, along with Beckett's testimony, was condemning evidence.

Beckett laughed to himself. The Fruitcake Lady was feisty, the kind of person you wanted in your corner. He owed her a great debt for saving his life. His thoughts went back to his dream of the woman in the snow. Even though he thought about her every single time he responded to a winter rollover call, it seemed like a different lifetime when he'd met her. She'd made him a deal—that she'd survive the accident if he got his life straightened out. His eyes grew misty as he swallowed. So many times, he'd wanted to track the lady down to tell her that he did indeed make good on his end of the deal.

He jerked, looking toward the door. For a split second, he thought his eyes were deceiving him—granting him the desire he most wanted. Ava.

Tears filled her crystal blue eyes, concern etched over her beautiful face as she rushed in. She paused for a second, giving him a tentative look, before dropping the items she was holding and flinging her arms around him. "Are you okay?"

He returned the hug, appreciating the softness of her hair as it tickled his nose. Joy swelled his heart as he took an assessment of his body. Miraculously, he'd not gotten burned. His head was sore, his eyes still burned from the smoke, and his lungs felt tight. He'd come out great considering the circumstance. He was so grateful to be alive, so grateful for another chance at life with this extraordinary woman. She pulled back, searching his face. "I'm glad you're okay."

An easy laugh slid from his lips. "Nothing that a few days of rest won't cure."

Her eyes hardened around the edges. "I can't believe Wesley would do such a thing."

He cocked his head. "How did you know about that? And that I was here?"

"Houston called me. He saw the fire on the news this morning, recognized your building. The video of Wesley and the woman has also been on the news. Houston told me about that too." She wrinkled her nose. "It's crazy. What're the odds that Wesley would get detained by some crazy lady while trying to flee the scene?"

A lopsided grin tugged at Beckett's lips. "Yeah, what are the odds?"

Ava gave him a funny look. "Do you know the lady?"

"Not well, but I've seen her a few times ... around." Someday, he'd tell Ava the full story. Right now, he wanted to just soak her in, savor the fact that she was here. Oh, and he had to set things straight between them. That was the first order of business.

She touched his cheek, tears glistening in her eyes. "When I got the call..." Her voice went hoarse as she swallowed. "Well, I was afraid I'd lost you." Time seemed to stop as she locked eyes with him. He was struck by how clear and beautiful her eyes were, like he could see forever in them.

He chuckled, a teasing grin tugging at his lips. "No danger of that," he drawled. "You're stuck with me."

Tears flowed down her cheeks, hope lighting her eyes. "Does that mean that you can forgive me? For not telling you everything from the beginning?" A pained expression overtook her features. "I should have. I'm so sorry. Please know that my love for you has nothing to do with the trust." Her voice quivered with intensity. "I promise you that from the depth of my heart."

"It was your choice, wasn't it? To leave me the trust?"

Ava rocked back, her jaw going slack. "Yes, it was." She shook her head. "H—how did you know?"

"I just know." He cupped her hands with his. "Everything's forgiven. For the record, I love you too." A wide smile filled her face. Beckett could've sworn it brought a ray of sunshine with it that shot into his heart, warming him down to his toes. He gave her a searching look. "I want to hear everything, from the beginning." He pushed out a laugh. "And, please, don't give me that drivel Houston did about me saving the girl from the fire." His eyes held hers. "I know there's more to it than that." His brows furrowed. "There has to be."

She swallowed, nodding. "Yes," she said simply.

He cocked an eyebrow, a goofy grin spilling over his lips. "Really?" He'd been playing hardball, fearing that maybe there wasn't any more to the story. Yet, he wanted there to be more. He wanted to understand Milton McQueen and what it was that he saw in Beckett.

She gave him a tender smile, tucking a strand of hair behind her ear. The subtle gesture sent warmth flowing through Beckett. Even the way she moved was intoxicating—so graceful and nimble. "Once you hear the full story, you'll understand why my grandfather left his trust to you." She pulled up a chair and sat down. Her eyes grew reflective as she took in a breath, pursing her lips. "Let's see," she mused, "where to begin. Remember when I told you about how my mother was killed in a car accident and how I went to live with my dad and grandparents?"

He nodded.

"I also told you I had two wonderful years with my dad before he died from his congenital heart defect." Sorrow touched her eyes, her lips vanishing into a thin line.

Beckett touched her hand, a swift river of sympathy rushing

through him. "You've been through so much ... I'm sorry." Briefly, he wished he could erase all the hurt from her life, then he thought better of it. Like him, Ava's struggles had made her the person she was, and Beckett wouldn't trade her for anything.

"Thanks," she responded softly. "I was raised by my grandparents, Milton and Sadie."

Beckett jerked slightly. "Sadie?" His throat went sandpaper dry. The room seemed to contract and expand, and he had the sensation of falling deeper into the bed. "Where did your grandparents live?"

"Ogden."

Beckett's mind whirled with the possibility. Could it be? He wound his hand around the blanket.

"My grandmother took it hard when my dad passed. He was her baby, the child she was closest to." Her voice took on a bitter edge. "Unlike Ted and Libby, my dad actually had a heart. Had he lived, I'm certain that my grandfather would've left him the trust." She drew in a deep breath, her eyes going distant. "Things would get bad for my grandmother around the anniversary of my dad's death. One snowy evening when my grandfather was at a business dinner, my grandmother took the car and went for a drive. The snow got worse, blizzard-like conditions. The roads were treacherous, my grandmother ran off the road."

Beckett drew in a sharp breath, the pieces of the puzzle fitting together. *Sadie, blizzard-like conditions, Ogden.* His jaw worked, emotion balling in his chest.

Ava bent down and reached for something at her feet. She handed it to him. Reflexively, he took it, not sure what he was holding at first. He looked down, inspecting it. Then, he let out a surprised gasp, tears rushing to his eyes. "My coat." His throat squeezed to the size of a straw as he pushed the words out. "The one I gave to the woman in the snow. Your grandmother was Sadie." Astonishment broke over him like a crashing tidal wave.

Tears dribbled down Ava's cheeks as she smiled tenderly. "She always spoke of the angel who saved her. If you hadn't come along, she would've died out there." She swiped at her tears, sniffling.

The corners of his lips came down. While he liked Ava thinking of him as a hero, he didn't want to take any undue credit. "That's not true. A car came along. The guy driving would've seen her."

"No, it would've been nearly impossible for anyone driving past to see her headlights. And she might have frozen to death or died of blood loss by then."

A comfortable silence settled between them, and Beckett knew Ava spoke the truth. He was the one who was supposed to find Sadie. That's why the Fruitcake Lady made sure he stayed on the bus. "The next day, I went to hospital after hospital to try and find Sadie. No one had a record of her ever coming in." His voice caught as he chuckled. "As the years passed, I wondered if I'd imagined the whole thing."

She squeezed his hand. "My grandfather pulled strings to keep it out of the media."

He looked at the amazing woman in front of him, who was fast becoming the focal point in his life. "That conversation with your grandmother changed my life." He swallowed to clear the emotion. "She was a brave woman." He laughed at the memory. "She told me she'd survive if I cleaned up my act."

"She did survive. She went on to live a couple more years." Ava paused, her lip quivering. "My grandfather often referred to those two years as the greatest gift of his life."

The rest came together like light flooding into a room after the curtains had been drawn. "Your grandfather sought me out at the park."

Her eyes glowed with an inner light. "Yes, he had the highest regard for you. He followed your life, was so impressed with how you overcame your demons. That was impressive to me too," she uttered, "especially after what happened to my mom." A thoughtful look came into her eyes. "Lots of people appear brave and put together, but it's only after going through the refiner's fire that you learn what you're truly made of." A sheepish grin tugged at her lips. "I admired you from afar, was influenced by my grandfather's admiration for you. After my grandfather died, I wanted to quietly observe the type

of man you were, on my own terms, before word of the trust got out."
She laughed ruefully. "That night at the bowling alley, I never
expected to meet you face-to-face." Her features softened. "I never
expected to fall in love with you."

Beckett's heart soared. He cupped her jaw. "I love you too." She
leaned in and gave him a long, tender kiss that sent a slow-burning
desire simmering through him. He could get lost forever in the feel of
her wonderful, insistent lips that fit so perfectly with his. He threaded
his fingers through her hair, pulling her closer. A groan of pleasure
sounded in her throat as the kiss deepened. Had he not been in the
wretched hospital bed and incapacitated, he would've pulled her into
his arms and given her a kiss that would've lit them both on fire.

A few minutes later, he pulled back and searched her delicate
face, marveling at how blessed he was. "Why did you do it?" He
rubbed a hand over her soft, silky hair.

She tipped her head, a bemused smile tugging at her lips. "Do
what?"

"Relinquish the trust to me."

She laughed lightly, the faintest trace of reproof swirling in her
captivating eyes. "All that glitters is not gold."

He choked on his saliva.

"Are you okay?" She touched his arm, flashing a look of concern.

He swallowed, clearing his throat. "Where did you hear that?"

She shrugged. "It's something my grandfather would often say
when referring to the most precious things in life. It's from
Shakespeare."

"Yes, I know," he murmured. A feeling of pure and undiluted joy
burst over Beckett as he let out a warm, throaty laugh. "I love you!"
The certainty of his words wrapped around him like a euphoric
cocoon. He'd finally found the right woman, his soulmate.

"I love you too."

He looked past Ava and saw the Fruitcake Lady standing in the
hall, peering in. Before he could get any words out, she tipped a smile
and gave him a salute as if to say, *Goodbye.* Somehow, in a way that

defied words, he knew he'd never see her again. "Thank you," he squeaked, emotion welling in his chest.

Ava frowned. "Who are you talking to?"

Beckett glanced at Ava. "To the woman in the hall." He smiled broadly. "Ava, there's someone I want you to meet."

As Ava turned around to look, Beckett also did the same. The woman was gone.

"No one's there." Ava made a face, turning back to him. "Are you sure you're okay?" Her voice faltered. "You're injured. Plus, I can't imagine how hard it must be for you. Losing everything in the fire. I'm so sorry."

He laughed, feeling deliriously happy. "On the contrary, I didn't lose anything." His eyes held hers. "I have Jazzie, my parents, ..." his voice grew soft "... you." He traced the curve of her cheek with the tips of his fingers. "You're everything I need."

"Right back at you," she uttered with an unencumbered laugh.

He wound a finger around a tendril of her fluid hair. "All that glitters is not gold," he murmured.

Ava rewarded him with a smile so brilliant that he thought he caught a glimpse of heaven. "Beckett Bradshaw, you're my gold," she said softly, leaning in for another kiss.

EPILOGUE

As Beckett stood looking at the shiny, new building in front of him, he couldn't help but feel blessed. In many ways, he felt like he was living a beautiful dream. Today marked a year from the date Beckett first learned he'd inherited Milton McQueen's trust. Sometimes it still felt surreal to think he was a billionaire. It had been a turbulent ride getting to this point. Once the media found out about the living trust, Beckett's entire life including his car accident and time on the streets, was broadcast over every internet site and TV channel known to man. The media frenzy had been especially hard on Jazzie, but she was tough and resilient. Pulling together, they'd made it through it. After several months, things settled back down to somewhat normal. Beckett chuckled. Was anyone's life ever really normal?

It had been more challenging than Beckett guessed to balance running a company with holdings all over the world and his job as a firefighter. These days, Beckett looked forward to his shift at the station, because it gave him time to clear his mind of the stress of McQueen Capital Management.

He grinned thinking about how floored the fire crew was when they learned about his inheritance. They teased him relentlessly, nicknaming him Daddy Warbucks. At first, Garrett expressed concerned that it would change the dynamics of the crew as well as bring undue attention to the fire department. However, thankfully, the media soon lost interest in Beckett and went on to the next story.

Beckett offered a smile and nod to the man walking towards him and Houston.

"Looks like it's about time for the show to start," Houston said, shoving his hands in his pockets, as he rocked forward on the balls of his feet.

As Scotty approached, he thrust out his hand to give Beckett a hearty shake. "Hey, Blanket Man." He motioned at the building. "It looks like you've built a fine shelter and training center. I'm honored that you're letting me run it for you."

"I can't think of a better man for the job," Beckett said, and he meant it. Scotty was compassionate to him when few other people were, taking the time to not only put aside the blankets for Beckett at the shelter, but also, talking to him like he was a person, not a number. Scotty truly cared about other people. That was the sort of man Beckett wanted on the frontline of this facility; which would provide people not only shelter and food, but also counseling and career training to help rebuild their lives.

"You must be decent at your job," Scotty teased. "Not bad for a firefighter turned real estate guru."

"Oh, he's more than good," Houston piped in. "This is the most profitable year we've ever had." He gave Beckett an appraising look. "I guess Milton McQueen was the smart one. He realized the boy was a genius when it comes to business."

"Thanks," Beckett said with a casual shrug, "but that might be laying it on a little thick." Houston had been right by his side the entire time, giving advice and being a sounding board. Not only was he a great mentor, but also a close friend.

Scotty pulled out his phone. "It's 10:15. What time is the media getting here?"

"The ribbon cutting ceremony is at 11:00," Houston said. "I reckon the posse will be arriving soon. The mayor's supposed to be here too."

He turned to Beckett. "What time are the missus and Jazzie getting here?"

"They should be arriving any minute." Even as Beckett spoke the words, Ava's BMW wagon pulled into the parking lot.

A few minutes later, Ava and Jazzie came into view. Ava's blonde tresses bounced against her red coat with her every step. She looked like a model with her perfect features and slender figure. Jazzie half-walked/half-skipped beside her. The two of them made up Beckett's entire world. Ava caught his eye and flashed a brilliant smile that caused his heart to flip. Having her as his wife was the greatest miracle in his life, besides Jazzie's recovery, proof that God wasn't keeping score of His blessings. Ava made Beckett the happiest man on earth when she agreed to become his wife. They were married the past June. The six months since had been the best in Beckett's life. Every single moment with Ava was an adventure, and he looked forward to a lifetime more.

"Sorry we're late," Ava began as she hugged Beckett. He leaned in and kissed her on the mouth. "You look beautiful."

"Thanks," she chimed, beaming.

Jazzie made a face. "Get a room," she said disgustedly.

Houston and Scotty let out a few surprised chortles.

Beckett shot Jazzie an exasperated look. "Really? The room thing again? I thought we'd been over this."

"Got ya!" Jazzie laughed, flashing Beckett an impish grin, letting him know the little stinker enjoyed razzing him. He grabbed her and ruffled her hair.

"Stop," she protested. "Dad, you're messing up my hair!"

"What're we gonna do with her?" he asked Ava.

Ava only smiled and shook her head.

"Just love me, I suppose," Jazzie said flippantly. "Oh, and I wouldn't mind having a new phone."

Beckett grunted. "Is that right?"

"Yes," Jazzie countered emphatically.

Now that Beckett had money, Jazzie's wish list was never ending. Yes, he could buy Jazzie everything her heart desired, but he wanted her to grow up responsibly, recognizing the value of work. That didn't stop the little stinker from asking for the world.

Jazzie turned to Ava, her expression pleading. "You know how badly I need a new phone." She brought her hands together. "Please."

"We'll talk about it," Ava said evasively, looking to Beckett for help. He only grinned, shaking his head. He was grateful that Ava and Jazzie got along so well.

"Also," Jazzie continued, "will we still be able to go to Disneyland after Christmas, even with a baby on the way?"

Beckett's jaw dropped. *Baby?* His pulse picked up its beat as he looked at Ava, whose face had turned as crimson as her coat.

"Jazzie," Ava exclaimed, her eyes widening. "You weren't supposed to say anything until I had a chance to talk to your dad." She gave Beckett a sheepish look. "I'm sorry, Jazzie saw the pregnancy test in the bathroom when we were getting ready." Her expression took on a radiant glow. "I just found out this morning."

Adrenaline shot through Beckett as his eyes misted. "Are you serious?"

A full smile broke over Ava's lips. "Yes." She gave him a tender look. "We're having a baby."

He let out a whoop and pulled her into his arms, twirling her around. "A baby!" He laughed, tears coming to his eyes. "That's wonderful!" he exclaimed. A feeling of overwhelming gratitude flowed through Beckett, making him feel like his heart would burst. He'd been the lowest of the low, a faceless homeless man who thought redemption was out of his reach. Then, in the most unexpected and wondrous way, a loving Heavenly Father had given him infinitely more than he could've ever hoped for. His cup was filled to overflowing.

"Congratulations," Houston said, giving him a hearty pat on the back.

"Yes," Scotty, added.

Beckett peered into Ava's eyes. "I love you," he murmured, stroking her hair.

Her lips tipped in a smile, revealing her adorable dimples. "I love you too."

He glanced at Jazzie, a teasing grin tugging at his lips. "You'd better close your eyes, Jazzie, because I'm about to give this wonderful woman of mine a kiss that will curl your toenails."

"Yuck!" Jazzie said with a mortified expression, but her eyes twinkled happiness.

Everyone else but Ava disappeared as Beckett's lips claimed hers. As a spark of desire flickered through his veins and their lips began their familiar dance, a single word kept running through Beckett's mind—joy!

WANT MORE CHRISTMAS ROMANCE? Check out Her Crazy Rich Fake Fiancé and Jennifer's Christmas Romance Collection.

YOUR FREE BOOK AWAITS ...

Hey there, thanks for taking the time to read *Yours By Christmas*. If you enjoyed it, please take a minute to give me a review on Amazon. I really appreciate your feedback, as I depend largely on word of mouth to promote my books.

If you sign up for our newsletter, we will give you one of our books, Beastly Charm: A contemporary retelling of beauty & the beast, for FREE. Plus, you'll get information on discounts and other freebies. For more information, visit:

http://bit.ly/freebookjenniferyoungblood

BOOKS BY JENNIFER YOUNGBLOOD

Check out Jennifer's Amazon Page:
http://bit.ly/jenniferyoungblood

Billionaire Boss Romance
Her Blue Collar Boss
Her Lost Chance Boss

Georgia Patriots Romance
The Hot Headed Patriot
The Twelfth Hour Patriot
The Unstoppable Patriot

O'Brien Family Romance
The Impossible Groom (Chas O'Brien)
The Twelfth Hour Patriot (McKenna O'Brien)
The Stormy Warrior (Caden O'Brien and Tess Eisenhart)
Rewriting Christmas (A Novella)
Yours By Christmas (Park City Firefighter Romance)
Her Crazy Rich Fake Fiancé

Navy SEAL Romance
> The Resolved Warrior
> The Reckless Warrior
> The Diehard Warrior
> The Stormy Warrior

The Jane Austen Pact
> Seeking Mr. Perfect

Texas Titan Romances
> The Hometown Groom
> The Persistent Groom
> The Ghost Groom
> The Jilted Billionaire Groom
> The Impossible Groom

Get the Texas Titan Romance Collection HERE
> The Perfect Catch (Last Play Series)

Hawaii Billionaire Series
> Love Him or Lose Him
> Love on the Rocks
> Love on the Rebound
> Love at the Ocean Breeze
> Love Changes Everything
> Loving the Movie Star
> Love Under Fire (A Companion book to the Hawaii Billionaire Series)

Kisses and Commitment Series
> How to See With Your Heart

Angel Matchmaker Series
> Kisses Over Candlelight
> The Cowboy and the Billionaire's Daughter

Romantic Thrillers
False Identity
False Trust
Promise Me Love
Burned

Contemporary Romance
Beastly Charm

Fairytale Retellings (The Grimm Laws Series)
Banish My Heart **(This book is FREE)**
The Magic in Me
Under Your Spell
A Love So True

Southern Romance
Livin' in High Cotton
Recipe for Love

The Second Chance Series
Forgive Me (Book 1)
Love Me (Book 2)

Short Stories
The Southern Fried Fix

ABOUT JENNIFER YOUNGBLOOD

Jennifer loves reading and writing clean romance. She believes that happily ever after is not just for stories. Jennifer enjoys interior design, rollerblading, clogging, jogging, and chocolate. In Jennifer's opinion there are few ills that can't be solved with a warm brownie and scoop of vanilla-bean ice cream.

Jennifer grew up in rural Alabama and loved living in a town where "everybody knows everybody." Her love for writing began as a young teenager when she wrote stories for her high school English teacher to critique.

Jennifer has BA in English and Social Sciences from Brigham Young University where she served as Miss BYU Hawaii in 1989. Before becoming an author, she worked as the owner and editor of a monthly newspaper named *The Senior Times*.

She now lives in the Rocky Mountains with her family and spends her time writing and doing all of the wonderful things that make up the life of a busy wife and mother.

facebook.com/authorjenniferyoungblood

twitter.com/authorjenn1

instagram.com/authorjenniferyoungblood

Made in the USA
Coppell, TX
21 August 2023